"Dorothea was so enthusiastic!" the vicar said at last. "Even in the photographs, that shines through. I felt I had only been half alive for years, that I'd wasted all the time before I knew her. I still can't believe that she agreed to marry me. I wrote to ask her, you know, as soon as I'd come home after that weekend. I couldn't sleep until I heard back from her. I don't know why she agreed. She said she had read my books and had admired me for years, but she was years younger than me. It was a wonderfully impulsive thing to do. I'm not surprised by her death, you know. Not after the first shock. It was all too good to last."

There was another silence.

"What about the parish?" Ramsay asked. "How did the church react to your new wife? Your marriage must have come as something of a shock."

"They loved her," Cassidy said quickly. "Everyone loved Dorothea."

Also by Ann Cleeves
Published by Fawcett Books:

A DAY IN THE DEATH OF DOROTHEA CASSIDY

Ann Cleeves

FAWCETT GOLD MEDAL • NEW YORK

A Fawcett Gold Medal Book
Published by Ballantine Books
Copyright © 1992 by Ann Cleeves

All rights reserved under International and Pan-American Copyright Conventions. Published in the United States by Ballantine Books, a division of Random House, Inc., New York, and simultaneously in Canada by Random House of Canada Limited, Toronto.

Library of Congress Catalog Card Number: 91-75842

ISBN 0-449-14789-4

Manufactured in the United States of America

First Edition: March 1992

1

Two boys found Dorothea Cassidy in
Prior's Park. It was June, Midsummer's Day. Although it was
seven in the morning, it had been light for hours. The boys
were on their way to begin a newspaper round and took a
shortcut as they always did along a footpath through the park.
Cycling was forbidden, but at that time in the morning there
was no one to complain. The boys were in high spirits. It
was the week of the midsummer carnival and they had spent
the evening before at the fun fair on the abbey meadow. They
were overtired, excited at the prospect of another night at the
fair. They shouted to each other, riding over the short grass,
and their tyres made tracks in the dew. The day was clear,
but there was still a remaining trace of mist over the River
Otter, winding through the ruins of the abbey and the spokes
of the ferris wheel on the opposite bank. Later it would be
hot.

The park was extensive and well laid out—coach parties
came from all over Northumberland to see the rose gardens.
The boys rode past the children's swings and the tennis courts
then followed the path along the river toward the centre of
town. Dorothea was lying in a border of flowers close to the
path. The border was still in shadow thrown by the tall trees
and shrubs beyond it, but even in the shade it would have

1

been impossible to miss her. She wore sky-blue dungarees and a knitted jacket in blues and golds. On her feet were sandals made of strips of red, plaited leather. Her hands were folded across her breast, so they could see her wedding and engagement rings against the brown skin of her long fingers. She was lying on her back, crushing the small plants beneath her, and despite the rich soil and the leaf mould, her face was quite clean.

The first boy braked sharply and there was almost a collision. They dismounted and stared, not believing what they were seeing. She looked like part of the design of the flower bed, surrounded by the brightly coloured and symmetrically patterned plants. The boys were fourteen and thought they were tough, but a regular diet of horror movies had not prepared them for the reality of sudden death. They looked around for adult help.

The younger boy came to his senses more quickly. He began to see the potential of the discovery. They might get their name in the papers, he said. It might even provide an excuse for a morning off school.

"Someone should stop here," he said, "and someone should fetch the police. Do you mind staying?"

The other shook his head. He could not take his eyes off the woman. He thought she was like a statue from a museum. Her skin was blue and looked very cold. He was tempted to touch her, almost expecting the hard, smooth surface of plaster or marble, but he knew better than to do that. He had heard about fingerprints. He watched Jamie pedal furiously away toward the town centre then turned back to her. He thought he had never seen anyone so beautiful. There must be something wrong with him, he thought. He must be really weird. How could anyone fancy a dead woman? He crouched protectively by the flower bed, watching her. A breeze from the river scattered the petals of a dying flower and one rested on her cheek like a tear.

2

When Inspector Stephen Ramsay was woken by the telephone, he expected the call to concern work. Who else would phone at six-thirty in the morning? Yet when he heard his aunt, speaking in such a loud, shrill voice that as he held the receiver at arm's length he was still able to hear her, he was not surprised. She had been widowed for twenty years but kept the same hours as when her husband had worked down the pit and needed a good breakfast inside him before he went out. She considered it a wickedness for anyone able-bodied to be in bed after seven in the morning. A wickedness and a waste.

"Well," she demanded. "Have you found her?"

Ramsay leaned across the bed and pulled open the curtains. The early sunlight made the trees on the other side of the dene seem very close and he could hear wood pigeons through the open window.

"I'm at home," he said mildly, "not at work. They hadn't done when I left last night."

"This is serious," she said. "She couldn't just wander off. Not Mrs. Cassidy."

"I know," he said. "We're taking it seriously." He had learned that it did no good to lose his temper with her. Her persistence was unaffected by anger. If he answered her questions, eventually she would leave him alone.

"Well," she said. "I hope you are. Everyone here's very upset."

She had her own flat in a sheltered housing scheme run by a local housing association. The move from the old coal board cottage had given her a new lease of life. She was into everything there, knew everyone's business. The other elderly residents held her in regard because she claimed a direct line to the police. They felt it gave the building special protection. She encouraged them in that belief and he had often been phoned at unwelcome times about missing pension books and the horror of dogs fouling the communal garden. He visited her once a week to have tea in the little overheated living room and quite often there would be a queue of residents waiting in the corridor to consult him as if he were the chiropodist. She would show them in one at a time and he would do his best to answer their questions and satisfy their demands.

Hunter, his sergeant, would mock the weekly visit to the old people's flats, but Annie had always been his favourite aunt, and despite the demands she made on him, he still felt a responsibility and an exasperated affection for her. When Stephen was a child, Annie had seemed less worn-out, less worn down than the other women he knew, perhaps because she had no children of her own.

There had been something theatrical about her. His mother had disapproved of her and said she showed off. Annie had been the provider of treats—the best seats at the pantomime at Christmas, picnics in the dunes at Druridge Bay—and while other adults' attempts to please often left him with a sense of anticlimax, her treats were as magnificent in the reality as in the expectation.

It was Annie Ramsay who had phoned him the evening before about the disappearance of Dorothea Cassidy.

"She was supposed to be speaking at our social club half an hour ago," she had said, as if it were his fault. "But she's not turned up."

"Give her a chance," he had said. "Perhaps she's ill or her car's broken down. Or got held up in the carnival traffic. You know what the roads are like this week. Perhaps she's just forgotten."

"Aye," Annie said. "Maybe. She's a bit of a reputation as a scatterbrain."

And Ramsay thought that with that he would be left in peace. But three quarters of an hour later Annie was on the phone again.

4

"She's still not here," she said. "I've just been in touch with her husband. He's not seen her since this morning. And if her car had broken down, she would have rung. She had this talk in her diary. I watched her write it down myself. You'll have to do something."

So Ramsay had done something. It hadn't been easy to persuade his colleagues in Otterbridge police station to take her disappearance seriously. There was the fair and the folk festival and they were all busy. But in the end they had listened. Other women might run off with their fancy men, get legless in Idols nightclub in Whitley Bay, and have to sleep it off on a friend's sofa before they dared to go home to their husbands, he said. But this was no ordinary woman. Dorothea Cassidy was a vicar's wife.

Sergeant Gordon Hunter had never found any reason to move out of his mother's house. It was comfortable there, and even when he was younger he had felt no need to establish his independence. She had never attempted to cramp his style. If he brought one of his girlfriends back to stay the night, his mother would make breakfast for them both the next day with her usual good humour. Gordon considered such attention only his due. He was an only child and had always been spoilt. Besides, since his father had left home to move in with the landlady of one of the roughest pubs in the town centre, his mother had no one else to look after. What else would she do?

His father's desertion had bewildered him. The pub was a dirty, run-down place, and when Gordon visited him there the man seemed exhausted. He helped in the pub after work carrying crates from the cellar, changing barrels, then sat, staring with besotted admiration at the ageing beauty behind the bar.

"She's wearing me out, lad," he would say. "And I love it."

5

Now, in the carnival week, the young men who travelled with the fair hung around the pub and there were reports of fights there every day.

"Serve him right," Gordon's mother said when she heard, but she did not care enough about her husband to wish him real harm. She was happy as she was and all the excitement she needed was provided vicariously by Gordon. Best of all, she liked to sit with her son in the evenings, drinking tea or sweet sherry while he talked about his work. She had few friends of her own and was immensely proud of him.

Early on June 21st Gordon Hunter went out for a run before work. He was very competitive, and when a colleague had bet him he couldn't complete the Great North Run, he had begun training seriously. Usually he found the daily run an effort, but on that Friday he enjoyed it. The weather was beautiful and the tidy gardens of the council estate where he lived were full of flowers. He moved easily and his breath came regularly. Two young women, factory workers in tight jeans and white overalls waiting at a bus stop, watched him with admiration and giggled appreciatively as he passed. When he returned to the house, he had to wait for a moment for his mother to let him in and he stood, running on the spot, hammering on the door and calling irritatedly for her to come.

"Sorry pet," she said. "I was on the phone."

She was soft, overweight, untroubled by anything. There was a smell of bacon and fried bread. She always had breakfast ready for him when he returned.

Hunter walked in, breathing deeply, shaking his hands to relax the muscles in his wrists.

"It was Mr. Ramsay," his mother continued. "He said could you phone him. It's urgent." Then in the same calm, conversational voice she added: "There's been a murder."

There were two entrances to Prior's Park. The first was close to the town centre by the road bridge which went over the

6

river into Front Street. That was large, with heavy wrought-iron gates, and was most often used. The second was small and discreet and led from an established residential area with quiet leafy streets. Now both entrances were blocked and policemen were turning away angry commuters who used the park as a shortcut to the town. Outside the main entrance two police cars were parked and a small crowd had gathered. Ramsay and Hunter had to push through the people and were watched with resentment as they strolled, unimpeded, into the park.

They walked down the footpath along the riverbank in the opposite direction to that taken by the boys earlier. The mist over the river had cleared and the sun was already hot. The constable who had been first sent to the scene stood by the body but nobody else had arrived. The three men stood at the edge of the footpath and looked down at the woman. The sun had risen above the trees and now her face was in sunlight. The colours of her clothes had the radiance of stained glass. Hunter whistled under his breath.

"She doesn't look like a vicar's wife to me," he said.

Ramsay said nothing. Annie had told him that Dorothea Cassidy was thirty-three and he trusted her abilities as an intelligence gatherer implicitly. Yet he had expected the woman to look middle-aged, dowdy, not only because she was a vicar's wife but because of her name, which he associated with women of his mother's generation. She did not look to him at all like a Dorothea. She was slim, taller than average, with high cheekbones and a wide mouth. Despite the bulging eyes and swollen tongue, which gave an indication of the cause of her death, he could tell that she had been lovely. Her short curly hair, protected from the soil by the crushed petals of the bedding plants, was copper coloured and had obviously been well cut. She wore silver earrings with a small blue stone and several silver bangles.

"What about the cause of death?" Hunter asked.

Ramsay looked at the blue tinge to the skin. "I think she was strangled," he said. "But we'll have to wait for the pathologist's report."

He crouched to look at the body from a different angle and saw a pink strip of sticking plaster on her left wrist. He lifted the hand gently.

"That looks recent," Hunter said. "Do you think it's important?"

Ramsay shrugged. How could he tell at this stage? He was tempted to make a sarcastic remark but said nothing. He supposed that he and Hunter should make some effort to get on.

By now it was the peak of the rush hour and they could hear the roar of traffic along the Newcastle Road beyond the trees.

"I wonder where she was killed." Ramsay was talking almost to himself. "She must have been put in that position. She didn't fall naturally with her arms folded like that. But if she was moved, it must have been immediately after death, before the onset of rigor."

"How did they get her here then?" Hunter said. "It's a fair distance from the road and she'd be no featherweight."

He thought it was all too contrived and elaborate. He preferred cases he could understand: a punch up in a bar, a jealous wife stabbing her husband. You knew where you were with cases like that. Here he suspected that nothing was as it seemed. It would suit Ramsay, Hunter thought bitterly. He liked things complicated, too.

"Then there's the question of time. . . ." Ramsay went on. "She was supposed to be speaking to the old folks at Armstrong House at seven-thirty. She couldn't have been put here then. The park would still be full of people. Someone would have found her last night even if the murderer could have got her here without being seen. So where was she all evening before she was killed?''

He turned to the uniformed constable, who seemed unable to take his eyes off the woman's face.

''Do they lock the park gates at night?'' he asked. ''Does someone check that the park's empty then?''

''They lock the main gate at sunset,'' the man said, ''but there's no way of blocking off the lane on the other side and they don't bother about that.''

''I suppose she might have been killed in the park then posed there in the flower bed,'' Ramsay said.

''Well, what was she doing here late at night all on her own then?'' Hunter said angrily. ''A woman like that. You'd have thought she'd have more sense.''

''A woman like what?'' Ramsay asked mildly.

''Well, man, you know. Respectable. The only people to come into Prior's Park after dark are courting couples and kids sniffing glue. You'd expect a vicar's wife to be inside watching the telly or''—he dredged his mind for a suitable activity for a vicar's wife—''knitting.''

Ramsay looked down again at Dorothea Cassidy. He looked at the wide mouth and imagined her laughing at the idea.

''She doesn't look the knitting sort to me,'' he said.

''It'll be one of those layabouts who travel with the fun fair,'' Hunter said definitely. ''They're all the same the gippos. There's always trouble when they're about. There was that rape two years ago when the fair was here.''

''We don't know that it was a sexual attack,'' Ramsay said. ''It doesn't look as if she's been raped. Not in those dungarees.''

''What about the husband?'' Hunter asked. ''Has he been informed yet?''

''No,'' Ramsay said slowly. ''I rather wanted to do that myself.''

"How did he seem last night when he knew his wife was missing?" Hunter asked.

Ramsay shrugged. "He wasn't too concerned apparently. Not at first at least. He said it wasn't unusual for her to be late. She wasn't naturally punctual, he said. She was easily distracted."

Hunter looked disapproving. "It seems a strange setup to me," he said. "You'd have thought she'd have to be home to get his tea."

Ramsay wondered briefly what Diana, his ex-wife, would have made of Hunter's views on the responsibilities of women. Ramsay had known from the beginning that she wasn't the sort of woman to wait at home to cook a policeman's tea, and her independence had nothing to do with the breakdown of her marriage. There was something about Dorothea Cassidy which reminded him of Diana, the mouth perhaps, and he turned suddenly away from her to speak to the constable who had been sent to identify the body because he was a regular member of Cassidy's congregation.

"Did she have any children?" he asked.

The man shook his head. Ramsay was surprised, relieved. He could picture her with a baby in her arms. Now who's being tempted into stereotypes? he thought.

"One of the first priorities is to find her car," he said. "It shouldn't be difficult. It's quite distinctive. A twenty-year-old Morris thousand estate. Her husband had it done up for her at one of those specialist garages as a present." He turned absent-mindedly towards Hunter. "Can you organise that?"

Hunter nodded and took out his radio.

"No," Ramsay said. "Go back to the station. There's no more to do here. I'll join you when I've seen the vicar."

Hunter walked off towards the bridge and the busy town, pleased at last to have something to do.

Ramsay knew that he would have to get to the vicarage quickly if he wanted to bring the news of Dorothea Cassidy's death to her husband. The tragedy would soon become general knowledge. Yet he found it hard to move away. Like the schoolboy who had found her, he was tempted to kneel and touch her. He turned towards the young constable, who stood now with his back to the body, staring blank-eyed across the river toward the abbey.

"What was she like?" Ramsay asked. "What did you think of her?"

The constable turned back to face the inspector, but he shook his head, too upset to speak.

In the large vicarage kitchen Edward and Patrick Cassidy sat facing each other and pretended to eat breakfast. There were reminders of Dorothea everywhere—in the plants on the deep windowsill, in the chaos of laundry in the basket on the washing machine, even in the scrubbed table which she had found in a junk shop in Morpeth and brought home strapped to the top of her car. Yet although both men were thinking of her, neither spoke of her directly.

"Where were you last night?" Edward Cassidy said abruptly.

Patrick looked up from his coffee, and for a moment his father thought he would refuse to answer. He had been so moody lately.

"I was at the fair," he said. If Dorothea had been there, he would have found it possible to explain why he had been drawn by the noise and the colour and the cheap, tacky prizes. He would have said that in the crowd he felt anonymous. It was a good way to escape. But Dorothea had disappeared and he knew he was responsible.

"On your own?" his father demanded, disbelieving.

How much does he know? Patrick wondered. How much did she tell him?

"Yes," he said sullenly. "On my own."

11

"I don't know what's going on!" Edward Cassidy cried. "Why isn't she here?"

Patrick looked at his father carefully, unconvinced by the outburst. He had been caught out by his father's histrionics before. Once Edward had confessed to him that as a young man he had ambitions to be an actor. "I would have been very good," he had said, laughing. "It isn't very different after all. Every sermon's a performance."

Patrick found the notion troubling, though it explained a lot. Did anyone know his father well? Perhaps even Dorothea had been taken in by him.

"I'm going to college," he said. "I'll be late."

The front doorbell rang and Edward leapt to his feet and rushed to answer it. Patrick watched without emotion, but moved to the kitchen door so he could hear what was going on.

It was Dolly Walker, the churchwarden's wife. Patrick recognised her middle-class, rather vague voice and heard his father immediately become charming. If Edward Cassidy had expected to find Dorothea at the door, he hid his disappointment well.

"I'm so sorry," he said. "Of course I knew the mothers' union wanted the parish hall this morning for the coffee morning. I should have opened it for you. I'll fetch the key."

Dolly did not ask if Dorothea would be there to help. She knew that Dorothea had no interest in either the mothers' union or coffee mornings.

Patrick went upstairs to his room to fetch books and bag. As he came down he hesitated by the telephone in the hall, but before he could make up his mind whether to make the call, the doorbell rang again and his father shouted from the study:

"That'll be Dolly Walker returning the key. Can you go?"

Patrick opened the door quickly. He would pretend to be in a hurry to reach the university, then there would be no opportunity for awkward questions about Dorothea. But instead of Dolly Walker with her blue silk dress and fluffy grey hair, there was a tall, stern man who stared at Patrick curiously and frightened him.

2

R*amsay* followed Hunter toward the town centre. As he walked along the footpath close to the water there was the smell of mud and vegetation from the river. Apart from the rumble of traffic in the distance the place was very quiet. No one had been allowed into the park and the usual cries of squabbling children, the inevitable hum of the motor mower were absent.

He reached the main road at eight-thirty. The church clock had just chimed the half hour. The bridge was clogged with cars tailing back from the traffic lights in Front Street. Between two lampposts across the road a large banner announced the Otterbridge Carnival and Folk Festival. Already he could hear some busker playing "Bobby Shaftoe" on a scratchy violin. All week the town had been full of strangers, filling the pubs to listen to the music, crowding into the fair on the abbey meadow. Tomorrow it would all be over and the clowns and mime artists and jugglers who held up the traffic and disrupted the routine of the town would be gone.

Ramsay spoke briefly to the policemen by the gate who were turning people away from the park then joined the crowd walking toward the town centre. Office workers in shirtsleeves crossed the road between stationary cars and sauntered on to their businesses. The shops were starting to open

14

and some owners were setting goods for display on the pavements. There had been good weather for weeks and the place had a continental air. Everyone Ramsay passed had a suntan, and in his dark suit he felt sober, pale, and overdressed.

The parish church was close to the river, next to the abbey ruins, at the end of a narrow street full of stylish boutiques, secondhand bookshops, and small restaurants. Outside the parish hall, on the other side of the street, well-dressed elderly women were carrying trays of cakes and scones from the boots of large cars.

They spoke in loud voices about the laziness of the caretaker who had failed once more to set out the tables as they had requested, and Ramsay thought with relief that they had not yet heard of Dorothea's death. The vicarage was behind the church, almost invisible from the street. Ramsay had never noticed it before. It was large, gloomy, with a wilderness of a garden. The stone was grimy and even in full sunlight it looked cold. Ramsay stood on the front step and rang the bell. The paint on the front door was beginning to peel in long strips, so the bare wood showed through.

The door was opened almost immediately by an athletic young man who seemed to be on his way out. He was dressed in jeans with patched knees, a dark T-shirt, and trainers. He seemed surprised to see Ramsay standing on the doorstep, as if he had been expecting someone else, and he stood for a moment staring, the door wide open behind him.

"Can I help you?" he said.

"I'm looking for Edward Cassidy," Ramsay said.

The young man continued to stare, and for a moment Ramsay wondered if this was the vicar. They wore jeans, didn't they, those trendy young priests the papers made so much fuss about? He realised immediately that this was impossible. The boy was eighteen or nineteen, too young to be a clergyman and too young to be married to Dorothea Cassidy.

"Yes," the boy said. "Of course I'll get him. Who shall I say it is?"

"Ramsay," the inspector said quietly. "Stephen Ramsay. But he won't know me."

He expected the boy to ask for more information, but perhaps he was used to strangers turning up on the doorstep.

"Yes," the young man said. "Right." He left Ramsay outside and disappeared down a long, dark corridor, yelling. "Dad, there's someone here to see you!"

The vicar must have asked if it was Dorothea because Ramsay heard the boy reply, "No, sorry. It's a man," in a tone that surprised Ramsay. There was no sympathy there.

Soon after, the boy returned. He was fair, sandy-haired, with the pale, almost transparent skin that freckles like a child's and strangely unblinking eyes.

"He'll be here in a minute," he said. "I'm in rather a hurry, I'm afraid, so I'll have to leave you to it."

Yet he lingered beside Ramsay on the doorstep. He was very thin and seemed to have an enormous, barely controlled energy.

"Oh," Ramsay said in a polite, interested way. "Where are you off to?"

"The university," the boy said, almost rudely, as if it were none of Ramsay's business.

Ramsay was surprised that he did not mention Dorothea. His stepmother had been missing all night. Hadn't he guessed that Ramsay was a policeman?

"I'm sorry," the inspector said apologetically. "I must ask you to stay at home this morning. I'm a police officer investigating the disappearance of Mrs. Dorothea Cassidy. I've some news for your father. I don't think he should be left alone today."

The boy stared in bewilderment as if he did not understand what the man was saying. Ramsay had expected him to ask questions, demand information, but he said nothing.

16

"If there's any problem with the university," Ramsay said, "I could always phone and explain."

"No," the boy said. "It's not that." He stood, loose-limbed, the sports bag still in one hand, and for a moment Ramsay thought he might volunteer information. He seemed on the brink of saying something important, then changed his mind.

"Look," he said. "I'll be in the garden if you need me." And he walked off to be swallowed up almost immediately by the overgrown shrubs and trees.

Ramsay walked slowly into the house and shut the door behind him, so that he was suddenly in shadow. After the stark sunlight of the garden he could make out little of the room, and when Edward Cassidy approached he was aware of him at first only because of the sound of firm steps on the wooden floorboards. Then his eyes grew accustomed to the shade and he saw a tall man, grey-haired, straight-backed, handsome. He must have been at least twenty years older than Dorothea, but he was still attractive. He looked after his appearance, Ramsay thought with irrational disapproval, as if it were wrong for a vicar to care what he looked like. He wore casual trousers and an open-necked shirt and had the same air of easy affability as a politician or a chat-show host.

"Yes?" Cassidy said. "How can I help you?" His voice was rich and without accent. He added, more uncertainly: "Is it about Dorothea?"

"My name's Ramsay. I'm from Northumbrian police. We talked last night."

"Yes, of course." Then, before Ramsay could continue: "What am I thinking of leaving you standing here? Come in and sit down."

He threw open a door and suddenly they were in a room full of light and colour. Sunshine flooded in through a long window. There was a shabby but richly embroidered chaise longue, a worn leather chesterfield with a red striped rug

17

thrown over the back, vases of dried flowers, paintings, photographs. Against one wall was a desk covered in books.

"Sit down," Cassidy said, and Ramsay was surprised because he seemed so calm, so determined to do the right thing.

"Do you know where my wife is?" the vicar asked. "You must have some news."

"Yes," Ramsay said. "I'm sorry." He paused. "She's dead. Her body was found early this morning in Prior's Park."

He looked at the clergyman, waiting for his response. Surely now he would lose his pose of considerate composure. Cassidy stared, his mouth open, almost ridiculous in his confusion.

"Dead?" he said. "How can Dorothea be dead? There must be some mistake. She was young, you know. Much younger than me." He shook his head in a gesture of disbelief. "I can show you a photo," he said, moving impulsively across the room. "That will prove that you're wrong."

"I'm sorry," Ramsay said, interrupting. "There's no mistake."

Still the priest seemed not to be convinced. He opened a drawer and pulled out a leather-bound photo album.

"One of our officers is a member of your congregation," Ramsay said. "He identified the body."

Cassidy stood quite still, clutching the photographs.

"How did she die?" he asked. "She never told me she was ill." The tone was almost petulant.

"There are suspicious circumstances," Ramsay said. "I'm afraid there will have to be questions."

"What sort of suspicious circumstances?"

"We're afraid," Ramsay said, "that she was murdered."

"No," Cassidy said. "That's impossible. Who would murder Dorothea?"

18

Yet still Ramsay thought that he was self-conscious, continually aware of the impression he was making. Perhaps performance was a habit and spontaneous response was impossible for him.

Then Cassidy sat down on a wooden chair with a curved wooden back close to the desk and put his head in his hands, and for the first time Ramsay thought he had stopped acting. But the gesture seemed not so much an indication of grief as an attempt to come to terms with the fact of his wife's death.

Ramsay sat still and quietly waited for him to recover. At last the man looked up.

"Can I see her?" he asked.

"Of course, but later. You understand that there are procedures, formalities."

"Yes," Cassidy said. "I understand." He was very pale.

"Do you feel ready to answer questions now? Can I fetch you anything?"

Outside the window in the garden the boy was struggling to set up an old-fashioned canvas deck chair on the long grass. Ramsay caught his eye, but Cassidy seemed unaware of his son.

"No," the priest said. "I don't need anything. Let's get on with it."

He crossed his legs and put his arms along the arms of the chair. Ramsay was for a moment ludicrously reminded of a *Mastermind* contestant waiting for the challenge of the questions.

"How long have you been married?" Ramsay asked. The question threw Cassidy and he paused. Perhaps he had been expecting something more specifically relevant to his wife's disappearance. Then he answered readily, almost with pleasure, as if the memory of their marriage and meeting brought him comfort.

"Three years," he said. "Almost exactly three years. Tomorrow would be our wedding anniversary."

19

Ramsay looked at the boy in the garden. He sat with books on his knees but seemed to make no attempt to work.

"You had been married before?" Ramsay asked.

"Yes." Cassidy moved a gold wedding ring on his finger. "Sarah, my first wife, died fifteen years ago after a long illness, cancer. Patrick was four then. It was such a blessing to have him with me. We became close and I thought that from then it would be just the two of us. Then I met Dorothea. I had never thought that happiness like that would be possible for me again. I lost my heart and all my senses."

He looked at Ramsay apologetically as if in the circumstances he should be excused such hyperbole.

"What did your son make of your marriage?"

"Patrick?" Again Cassidy seemed surprised, as if he had been so wrapped up in his relationship with Dorothea that he had hardly considered his son. "He was pleased for me. By then he was quite independent, you know. He came to admire her tremendously."

Ramsay paused. He knew that Hunter would have structured the interview quite differently, going immediately for the facts, demanding information about her movements, her friends, but he had decided that Dorothea Cassidy was an unusual woman and he wanted to know more about her.

"Where did you meet your wife?" Ramsay asked. "Was she a member of your congregation?"

"No," Cassidy said. "She was the cousin of one of my college friends. I met her quite by chance when I went to Cornwall to visit him for a weekend."

Even in his grief, his excitement at the meeting was obvious.

"She was working then for a Christian aid agency and had just come back from a spell overseas. . . . You can't know what it was like."

He turned in his seat and from under a pile of papers he drew a leather-bound photograph album.

20

"Look," he said. "This is how I first saw her. I took this photograph in Cornwall." Ramsay stood up and moved over to the desk. Cassidy pointed to a picture of Dorothea on a beach. She was sitting on a large boulder, her head thrown back, laughing into the camera. The wind blew her hair away from her face.

"It was early March," Cassidy said. "One of those breezy, sunny days. The three of us went for a walk. . . ."

He continued to turn the pages and Ramsay saw Dorothea at their wedding, stately and elegant in white, then at the Sunday school picnic in Prior's Park, surrounded by children, then in the vicarage garden with Patrick on one side of her and a pale blond girl on the other, her arms round them both.

"That's Patrick's girlfriend, Imogen," Cassidy said. "It was his birthday. Dorothea cooked a meal for us all. . . ."

The images suddenly seemed too painful for Cassidy and he shut the album. Ramsay returned to his seat. He said nothing. He felt that Cassidy wanted to talk about his wife, and if he waited, the words would come.

"Dorothea was so enthusiastic!" the priest said at last. "Even in the photographs that shines through. I felt I had only been half-alive for years, that I'd wasted all the time before I knew her. I still can't believe that she agreed to marry me. I wrote to ask her, you know, as soon as I'd come home after that weekend. I couldn't sleep until I heard back from her. I don't know why she agreed. She said she had read my books and had admired me for years, but she was years younger than me. It was a wonderfully impulsive thing to do. I'm not surprised by her death, you know. Not after the first shock. It was all too good to last."

There was another silence.

"What about the parish?" Ramsay asked. "How did the church react to your new wife? Your marriage must have come as something as a shock."

21

"They loved her," Cassidy said quickly. "Everyone loved Dorothea."

"In my experience," Ramsay said, "change is never universally welcomed."

Surprisingly Cassidy smiled. "Of course you're right," he said. "St. Mary's has always been considered conservative and some of the elderly parishioners found it hard to adjust to a new situation. When I was first ordained, I had the reputation, through my looks, of being something of a rebel, but over the years I've learned the value of compromise and tolerance. Dorothea had strong views and always found compromise difficult."

"So she ruffled a few feathers?"

"I suppose so," Cassidy said. "Not deliberately, of course. She never set out to shock. I don't think she even realised the reaction she provoked."

"That must have put you in a difficult position," Ramsay said.

"Perhaps," Cassidy said. "I don't like unpleasantness, bad feeling. It seems unnecessary. Occasionally I thought I should have supported her more strongly, but I didn't want to offend. Some of the church council had a misleading impression of our relationship. They saw me, I gather, as a henpecked husband who had been bullied to accept new ideas."

"Was that true?" Ramsay asked. "Were you in sympathy with your wife's views?"

"Oh yes. Completely. All the same, I could understand the distress that change can bring to people who hold very traditional views."

So you sat on the fence, Ramsay thought. He had known senior police officers like the clergyman. They took all the credit when things were going well, but denied responsibility if there was criticism.

"Perhaps you could explain the changes which were specifically objected to," he said. "It's hard for an outsider to understand."

"Oh," Cassidy said. "There was nothing specific, you know. It was more a difference in attitude, in perspective."

Then Ramsay decided that he would have to learn the substance of any disagreement between Dorothea and the elderly parishioners from someone else and that it was time to change the direction of the questions.

"When did you last see your wife?" he asked.

"Yesterday morning," Cassidy said. "The three of us had breakfast together."

"Was it unusual for your wife to be out all day?"

"Not on a Thursday. She had trained to be a social worker and Thursday was her day for voluntary work. Sometimes she managed to get home for lunch, but I didn't really expect her."

"Did you know that she had planned to give a talk to the old people at Armstrong House in the evening?"

"I don't know. I suppose so. I mean I expect she told me, but I don't quite remember. She was so disorganised, you know, always brimming with new projects. Thursday was *her* day, you see. I didn't interfere. Quite often she arrived home late in the evening after a meeting, sometimes she went out with her friends for a meal. She said that it was important for her to have one day when she felt she really achieved something. It wasn't always easy to organise, but I could understand why she needed it. . . ."

He trailed off and sat again with is head in his hands. Ramsay said nothing, and as the silence grew he could sense Cassidy's discomfort. The man had loved his wife, but he wanted Ramsay to understand that living with her had not always been easy.

"Sarah was very much a traditional vicar's wife," he said. "She ran the mothers' union, saw to the flowers. You know the sort of thing. Dorothea had other gifts."

23

There was self-pity in his voice. He made it clear that Dorothea's gifts had been to him a mixed blessing. "She was very concerned that we should attract young people into the church and was convinced that we should make the worship more accessible to them. A lot of her energy was directed in that direction. She started a youth club, for example, and organised the crèche during family communion. But she had so many enthusiasms that she was still unfulfilled. She needed her Thursdays."

"Yes," Ramsay said. "I see." But what did she get up to? he wanted to say. What did she do on Thursdays that so fulfilled her? Instead he said: "Did she work with any one organisation? The social services department? Probation?"

Cassidy shook his head. "Nothing like that," he said. "Though she worked very closely with them both. She saw herself as a catalyst, setting up new projects, encouraging other people to help themselves."

"Did she have a diary?" Ramsay asked. "You can see that it's vital that we find out where she went yesterday."

"Yes," Cassidy said. "It was one of those big page-a-day affairs. She was always losing it and throwing the whole house into panic. Her memory was appalling and she wouldn't have survived without it."

"What about a handbag?" Ramsay asked. "We didn't find one with her."

"Yes, though it was too big really to be called a handbag. She had brought it back from Africa. It was made of brown leather with an embossed pattern of birds on the flap. She was very fond of it."

For the first time in the interview Ramsay wrote in his notebook.

"And you have no idea at all where she might have gone yesterday?" he said. "Did she have any regular Thursday appointments?"

24

But Cassidy only shook his head sadly and absentmindedly. He stood up and walked to the window and looked out at his son.

"I must ask you some questions about your movements last night," Ramsay said. "You do understand. In a murder enquiry we have to take statements from everyone."

"Yes," Cassidy said. "Of course." He still seemed preoccupied with his son.

"Where were you yesterday evening? Perhaps we could start at about five and go on until this morning."

"This morning?" Cassidy said. "But Dorothea went missing at seven-thirty yesterday evening. Annie phoned from Armstrong House to tell me."

"We think she must have been murdered rather later than that," Ramsay said. "Though of course we'll have to trace her movements to find out where she was in the early evening. So, where were you at five o'clock?"

"I was here in the vicarage, but only until about quarter past," Cassidy said. "From half-past five until half-past seven I was in the cottage hospital visiting the patients. Most of them are geriatric and many are quite confused, but they seem to welcome the visit. It's a regular commitment. I go every week."

"Then Dorothea could have returned to the vicarage during that time without you knowing?"

"I suppose so. Patrick might have been in, of course, at least for some of the time."

"But there was no indication that she had been in the house? No sign, for example, that she had prepared herself a meal?"

"No," Cassidy said. "I don't think so, though if she had just made coffee and a sandwich, I probably wouldn't have noticed."

"What time did you return from the cottage hospital?"

25

"At about a quarter to eight."

"Was your son here then?"

"No," Cassidy said. "He had come home from the university, but he'd gone out again. He has a very active social life. I find it hard to keep up with him."

"Soon after you arrived home Annie Ramsay phoned from Armstrong House to say that Dorothea hadn't turned up for the talk?"

"Yes," Cassidy said. "That must have been at about eight o'clock."

"Were you concerned?"

"Not at first. To tell the truth, I was a little irritated. Dorothea was sometimes so busy that she overcommitted herself. I presumed that she was late because aprevious appointment had taken longer than she had expected."

"Did you go out to look for her?"

"Not then. I had arranged for a young couple who plan to marry in St. Mary's to come to see me. They came at half-past eight and stayed for about twenty minutes. By then I was starting to be a little worried about Dorothea. Usually if she was that late, she phoned me, and it was unlike her to miss an appointment altogether. I phoned some of her friends but no one had seen her. At about ten o'clock I went out to look for her."

"Did you have any idea where to look?"

"None at all. It was hopeless. With the fair and the festival there was traffic everywhere. I'd planned vaguely just to drive round the bypass in case her car had broken down, but it all took much longer than I anticipated.

"It was a foolish thing to do, but I felt so helpless, just waiting here on my own. I suppose I just hoped that when I returned, she would be here waiting for me with some perfectly reasonable explanation for why she'd gone missing. . . ." He paused. "It happened once before, you know,

26

after an argument, one of those trivial arguments that develop out of nothing. We both lost our tempers and said some unpleasant things. Dorothea left the house and didn't come back all night. Patrick and I were frantic with worry. At dawn I went out to look for her, and when I came back, she was here, sitting at the kitchen table as if nothing had happened, drinking coffee. She offered to make me breakfast. Later, when I asked her where she had been, she said it didn't matter. She had needed to be on her own, a time almost of retreat. She hadn't realised, I think, how anxious I would be."

"But yesterday there was no argument?"

"Oh no," Cassidy said. "There was nothing like that."

"Yet you didn't contact the police."

"No," he said sharply. "Dorothea would have been furious if there had been any fuss. Thursday was *her* day, and I'd promised not to interfere. The police did phone, when I got back, to see if I'd heard from her. Apparently Annie Ramsay had alerted them."

"What time did you return from your search for her?"

"I'm not sure. Perhaps half-past eleven."

"Was your son back then?" Ramsay asked.

"No," Cassidy said sadly. "The house was still dark. I went to bed in the end. There seemed nothing else to do. Patrick came in at half-past twelve. I heard his footsteps on the drive and looked out of the bedroom window in case it was Dorothea. He saw me and waved, but we didn't speak."

There was a silence and then Cassidy said simply: "I'd like to be on my own for a while now, Inspector. I'm sure you understand. If you have any more questions, you can come back later."

"Of course," Ramsay said. "There's just one more thing. Had Mrs. Cassidy cut herself when she left home yesterday morning? Perhaps there was some accident? There appears to be a wound on her wrist.''

Cassidy seemed confused.

''No,'' he said. ''There was nothing like that. I'm sure I should have noticed.''

Ramsay thanked him and left him alone in the room that was full of memories of his wife.

3

Patrick Cassidy was in love, and from the beginning that clouded his judgement. Later he was amazed at his own stupidity. He should have realised at once that Ramsay was an intelligent man who needed careful handling. He should have thought the thing through more clearly. His mistakes came, he saw afterwards, from an inflated idea of his own importance. He should have used that time in the garden while Ramsay was talking to his father to prepare his story. Instead, when the inspector came out of the house and sat beside him on the grass, he was confused and uncertain.

Ramsay, too, was feeling his way. Apart from his work he had little contact with young people. He distrusted them and envied their freedom and irresponsibility. He was not sure how to talk to them. Patrick Cassidy had flattened a path in the long grass between the house and the patch of open sunlight where he sat. As he walked along it Ramsay could feel the boy looking at him, and he was nervous, too. The vicarage garden backed onto the river, though the water was hidden by the shrubbery beyond the lawn. Cassidy's wait, the night before, must have been accompanied by the music of the merry-go-round in the fun fair along the bank. On the opposite shore the pathologist and the scene-of-crime team

29

would be looking at Dorothea's body. From an upstairs window it might be possible to see them.

When Ramsay reached Patrick Cassidy, the boy stood up, not, it seemed, because of an old-fashioned respect for authority, but because he found it impossible, any longer, to sit still.

"Please," Ramsay said. "Sit down." He took off his jacket and sat on the grass, then he did not know how to continue.

"What are you doing here?" the boy asked. "Where is Dorothea?"

"I'm sorry," Ramsay said. "Your stepmother is dead."

Patrick Cassidy did not move. It was as if he had been winded by a heavy blow. Ramsay was sure the news came as a surprise to him.

"Yes," he said at last. "Of course. I should have known."

"Should have known what?"

"That she was dead. When she wasn't here this morning. I should have realised."

"I'm sorry," Ramsay said. "I don't understand."

The boy shook his head in confusion. "I had thought that there might be some other reason for her staying away. Perhaps one of us had upset her without realising. But that was foolish. She and Dad were happy."

He spoke quickly, without emotion. The sun had made his face red, and as he leant forward in the chair his blue eyes stared out with unnatural intensity.

"What happened?" he demanded. "Was it the car?"

"No," Ramsay said. "It wasn't the car. We believe that she was murdered."

"Who killed her?" the boy asked very quietly, and again he was quite still, as if he were holding his breath.

"We don't know," Ramsay said. "Not yet."

"Where was her body found?"

30

"Here in Otterbridge. In Prior's Park, close to the river." That seemed almost to bring him some relief.

"Prior's Park," he repeated. "What was she doing there?"

"We don't know," Ramsay said. "I'm here to ask questions. We need to trace her movements."

"Yes," Patrick said. "Of course. I'm sorry. When you said she was dead, I thought there must have been an accident. She drove that bloody car like a maniac." He turned to face Ramsay. "It must have been a stranger," he said. "No one who knew Dorothea would have wanted to kill her."

"She had no enemies then?" Ramsay asked mildly. "I understood from your father that she wasn't always popular in the church."

"Oh!" Patrick said. "Those malicious old biddies were harmless enough. They might stab you in the back figuratively but not literally."

"Mrs. Cassidy was strangled, not stabbed," Ramsay said quietly.

Patrick went pale, and for a moment Ramsay thought he would be sick.

"I'm sorry," the boy said. "It was just a manner of speaking. I didn't realise."

"No," Ramsay said. "How could you?"

There was a silence. Patrick stood up and looked down at the policeman.

"She wasn't frightened of dying, you know," he said. "We talked about it once. She was the sort of person you could discuss anything with. How could she be? she said. I think that's why she drove the car so recklessly. She wasn't frightened of anything."

"When did you last see her?" Ramsay asked.

The boy paused. "Yesterday morning at breakfast. Dad was there, too, hiding behind his newspaper, waiting for us to go so that he could have the place to himself. Dorothea

31

was in a rush, disorganised as usual. She had half a bowl of meusli and a glass of orange juice. And lots of coffee. She was a coffee addict. She offered me a lift to the station. I usually get the train into town—but she was obviously in a hurry and I said I'd walk.''

"Did she tell you what her plans for the day were?''

"No,'' Patrick said. "I don't think so. Not in any detail.'' He remembered the meal, the strain between them, Dorothea's demands for information and his refusal to give it. And throughout it all his father sitting oblivious reading the *Telegraph*. Then he remembered that in the end his father had lowered the paper and there had been a conversation of sorts, with Dorothea doing most of the talking.

"Something was worrying her,'' he said, because he wanted to tell the policeman something. "A case conference. 'I hate the idea of taking a child into care,' she said, 'and this time I'm not even convinced that it's necessary.' '' He looked down at Ramsay. "I'm sorry,'' he said. "I wasn't really listening.'' And that was true, he thought. He had other things on his mind.

"Thank you,'' Ramsay said. "That's very helpful.'' A case conference meant that Dorothea Cassidy had been involved in something official. A case conference meant social workers and teachers. It should be easy enough to find out where that had taken place. "Did you see your stepmother again during the day?'' he said. "Or her car?''

Patrick hesitated, and for the first time Ramsay wondered if he might be lying. He seemed for a moment to panic, but when he spoke at last, he was calm enough.

"No,'' he said. "I was in Newcastle all day. At the university.''

"What time did you get home?''

"At about five-thirty. I came on the bus.''

"Was anyone in the house when you arrived?''

32

"No," Patrick said very quickly. "It was Dad's evening for the cottage hospital."

"And no sign of Dorothea?"

"If there had been," Patrick said firmly, "I would have already told you."

"Yes," Ramsay said absently. "I'm sure you would."

The boy sat down again on the deck chair and curled in it to face the policeman.

"I can't help you," he said. "I'm sorry."

"All the same," Ramsay said mildly, "I have to ask the questions. I'm sure you understand. What time did you leave the house again?"

"Just after seven."

"How did you spend the time in the house?"

The boy shrugged as if this were all a waste of time, but Ramsay could sense his discomfort and persisted. "Please answer, Mr. Cassidy."

"I had a shower and changed," Patrick said. "There was some ham and salad in the fridge. I helped myself to that."

"Were there any phone calls?"

"Two," Patrick said. "Both for Dad. They said they'd phone back later."

"Did they leave their names?"

"No."

"Where did you go when you left the house at seven o'clock?"

"Just into the town," Patrick said.

"Were you with friends?"

"No," Patrick said, perhaps too quickly. "Most of my school friends have left the town now and the people at the university don't like leaving Newcastle."

"So you were in Otterbridge from seven o'clock until past midnight on your own? What did you do?"

"I like it here at carnival time," Patrick said defensively. "I went into a couple of pubs where there was live music. I

33

thought I might bump into someone I knew, but it was so crowded . . . you could be a couple of feet from your grandmother and not realise.''

"Where exactly did you do?'' Ramsay asked, and Patrick named two pubs in Front Street.

"Did you come straight home when the pubs closed?''

"No.'' Patrick looked embarrassed. "I went to the fair.''

Again he would have liked to explain the attraction of the oily machines and the childhood smells of hot dogs and candy floss, but he said nothing. Ramsay found the boy's explanation of his evening plausible and frustrating. It provided no sort of alibi, yet it was impossible to disprove.

There was a pause and Ramsay got awkwardly to his feet.

"Is there a friend's house, where you and your father could spend the day?'' he asked. "The press will soon come to hear of your stepmother's murder and you'll be rather accessible at the vicarage. I think your father deserves one day's peace.''

"Yes,'' Patrick Cassidy said. "I'm sure there is—''

He was interrupted by Edward Cassidy, who appeared at the kitchen door. Patrick crossed the grass and stood by his father in the shadow of the house, but they did not touch. Ramsay thought that the priest had been crying and wondered if his faith could be any comfort at a time like this. It was beyond his understanding.

"I've suggested that you stay with a friend for the day,'' Ramsay said, "to avoid the press.''

"I don't know. . . .'' Cassidy said. He seemed older, incapable of making decisions.

"I'll take you,'' Patrick said. "We'll go to the Walkers in your car.'' He turned to Ramsay. "Major Walker is the churchwarden,'' he said, "His wife is in the hall. Could you see if it's all right?''

Ramsay nodded, but before he could leave, the priest touched his arm.

34

"You will keep in touch? Let me know when I can see her?"

Ramsay nodded again. "Would you mind if I had a look around the house while you're out?" he said. "There may be something which provides a clue to where your wife was yesterday."

He thought for a moment that the man would object, but he seemed too weak to resist.

"No," he said at last. "I don't mind."

Then, for the first time Patrick reached out and put his arm round his father's shoulder and helped him through the house to the car, where they waited for Ramsay to return.

It was ten o'clock and the doors of the parish hall had just been opened to allow the public into the coffee morning. There was an unruly crowd around the cake stall and a more orderly queue at the counter, where a flushed woman hovered anxiously over a tea urn. It was clear to Ramsay that the news of Dorothea's death had reached the mothers' union. Among the helpers there was a troubled silence. Some thought they should conceal the whole event, but no one was willing to take the decision. He found Dolly Walker in the kitchen. She had been weeping and the mascara ran in streams down her face.

Of course the Cassidys must spend the day with them, she said. They could stay as long as they liked.

Ramsay took details of the address and phone number and watched her scurry away to prepare the house for them, glad of the excuse to grieve in private, secretly gratified that she had been selected for the honour.

At the vicarage the men still sat in the car in silence. Ramsay stood at the front door and watched them drive away. With the departure of the Cassidys the house seemed very quiet. He walked round and entered through the backdoor, through a dark scullery and a large and comfortable kitchen.

He had no real idea what he hoped to find—perhaps some letters belonging to Dorothea which would give a clue to how she spent her Thursdays. Perhaps a more vivid impression of how the three of them had got on together in this large and daunting house. He wondered suddenly why Dorothea had decided to marry Cassidy and take the whole thing on after one brief meeting on a windy Cornish beach. Was there something romantic in her nature which made the impulsive decision appeal to her. Or was it like everything else she did, a matter of faith?

He went first to the small room where Cassidy had showed him the photographs. The couple must both have used it as a study. Ramsay thought Cassidy would see his parishioners here amid the chaos. It would prove to them how busy he was.

Ramsay went to the desk and sorted the paper there into two piles—that belonging to Dorothea and that to Edward Cassidy. On Edward Cassidy's pile there were letters about the routine running of the church—quotations for a new heating system, a query about St. Mary's contribution to the Church Urban Fund. There were also several articles, all unfinished, meant apparently for the religious press. On a small bookcase was a row of Cassidy's books. The photograph on the back jacket was of a much younger man, and Ramsay found that the most recent had been published fifteen years before. Cassidy, it seemed, had a major writer's block.

On Dorothea's pile there were letters from friends—long, intimate letters in a variety of styles of handwriting, asking for advice, sharing problems. Then there were photostated circulars asking the couple to pray for a number of different projects including a missionary school in Tanzania, the Amazon rain forests, and a new minibus for a church in Birmingham. What a responsibility! Ramsay thought. Did they expect her to solve the world's problems single-handed? On the top of the desk was a large brown envelope which had a British postmark but which contained a batch of drawings and carefully printed notes from the children in the orphanage which she had supervised when she had been working overseas. Ramsay presumed that it had been brought back by a member of staff on leave, then posted. It had been sent on the 19th of June, so Dorothea must have received it the day before and opened it before disappearing to the town. Ramsay spread the brightly coloured crayoned pictures over the desk. One said in large and wobbly letters: *Come back soon.*

The other downstairs rooms were large and unfriendly. They smelled rather damp, although the spring had been warm and sunny, and Ramsay thought for the first time that the family could not be well off. The kitchen and study would be cheaper to heat in winter. There was a dining room with an ugly table and six chairs and a living room containing almost a dozen shabby armchairs set around the walls, which could only have been used for parish meetings. Ramsay felt that they had nothing to do with Dorothea, and after a brief search he shut the doors.

Upstairs, the first room he came to was the Cassidys', and here the sense of Dorothea was everywhere—in the brightly coloured rug which covered the large, low bed, in the African wall hangings and the wood carvings standing on the mantelpiece. Her clothes were still thrown over the chair by the window—there was a cream calico skirt and blouse—and on the dressing table there was a mess of her makeup, perfume, a pile of cheap bangles, and brightly enamelled earrings. On the floor by the bed were the books she had been reading—a magazine called *Third World Review*, a David Watson, and an old Penguin detective story with cream-and-green covers.

The room was at the back of the house and from the window there was a view of the garden—on the lawn the deck chair still stood where Patrick Cassidy had left it—then on to the river and Prior's Park on the opposite bank. Ramsay could see quite clearly the blue-and-white tape his colleagues were using to mark the area they were searching. If it had not been for a row of screens, he would have been able to see the body.

After the profusion of colour in the main bedroom Patrick's seemed bare. There were none of the posters of rock stars which Ramsay associated with teenage rooms and the record collection was small and old, as if he had gone into music once, when he was younger, but dismissed it as not for him. Why then, Ramsay wondered briefly, had he been so interested in the folk music the night before?

There *were* lots of books neatly set in rows on a home-made bookcase of breeze blocks and chipboard. Patrick must be reading English literature at university, Ramsay decided. The shelves were filled with titles the inspector had heard of but never read. A small square table which acted as a desk was set against one wall and on it was a copy of Gerard Manley Hopkins and a translation of Aeschylus. There was also a plastic-covered ring file which Ramsay opened idly, expecting to find notes on the books the boy had been reading. Instead there were about a dozen loose-leaf pages, each containing an example of Patrick Cassidy's own verse. The poems were obscure and intense and Ramsay guessed that they were probably bad. But as he read one after another it became clear that Patrick Cassidy was passionately and desperately in love. The object of the infatuation was, Ramsay supposed, the blond girl in the photo downstairs. The poems were strangely joyless and despairing, and he wondered what sort of masochism tied the boy to a woman who gave him so little pleasure.

Thankfully Ramsay shut the folder and went out onto the landing. The three spare bedrooms were dusty, the furniture large and old-fashioned. One had bare floorboards. Ramsay walked slowly downstairs. The phone began to ring loudly.

He found the telephone on a small table in the hall and answered it.

"Yes?" he said.

"Could I speak to Patrick, please?" It was a young woman, breathless, anxious. Perhaps this was the object of Patrick Cassidy's affection.

"I'm sorry," he said. "Patrick's not here at the moment. Can I take a message?"

But she had already replaced the receiver.

Outside in Front Street two clowns on stilts were entertaining the morning shoppers and someone with a megaphone was shouting that this was the last day of the festival and the grand parade would be held tonight. After the cool of the vicarage it seemed very hot.

On his way into the police station Ramsay bumped into Gordon Hunter, who was making a great show of being in a hurry. There had just been a phone call, Hunter said. Some old boy had found Dorothea Cassidy's car parked in his drive.

4

W*alter Tanner* did not find Dorothea Cassidy's car, parked in the drive of his modest, semidetached house, until nine-thirty that morning. Since his retirement he had indulged himself in the mornings with breakfast television and several cigarettes before even leaving his bedroom. He was ashamed of his laziness but, as with his other secret vices, found he could do little to change.

He saw the car as he drew the living-room curtains and thought for a moment it was some monstrous prank. Then he expected to see Dorothea Cassidy herself on the doorstep.

"What nonsense will it be this time?" he said out loud to give himself courage. He was St. Mary's second churchwarden, secretary of the parochial church council, and since her arrival she had taken to dropping round, uninvited. She seemed to need no excuse, though he could guess why she wanted to see him today. She said it was useful for her to discuss her ideas with him. He had so much experience, she said. So much to *give*. Then she would fix him in her gaze and launch into her plans for some new scheme. Last month's enthusiasm had been the formation of a liturgical dance group. Even now the thought of it gave him a sick, lightheaded feeling, which had nothing to do with having eaten no breakfast.

"What would they wear?" he had asked, to give himself time.

"I don't know," she had said. "I hadn't really thought about it. Something loose and expressive, I suppose. Or leotards. And bare feet."

"Bare feet!" The words had seemed to him to reflect all that was wrong with the present state of the church he had been brought up with. They represented a denial of the ritual and majesty of the Book of Common Prayer. They made him think of mothers feeding babies on the back pew, toddlers frolicking around the altar, and hymn numbers being called out bingo fashion to disrupt the rhythm of the worship.

Dorothea had smiled at him, apparently unaware of his horror. Was she really so innocent, he wondered, that she could not guess the extent of his disapproval? Surely these visits were only part of her plan to get her own way. Yet, alone in her presence, he found it impossible to doubt her good intentions. When she brought up her plans at the PCC meeting, he found it easy to discuss them with righteous indignation. The old forms of worship had held the church together for hundreds of years, he said. They shouldn't abandon them in a misguided attempt to be fashionable. But confronted in his own home by Dorothea's idealism, he found his hostility harder to express. He was frightened that without the security of the familiar words of the old service, his faith would fall apart, and how could he tell her that? She was so intimidating in her certainty.

"I don't see how I can help you," he had said. "Church wardens have no real power, you know. Edward is the vicar. You should discuss your ideas with him."

"Ah, Edward," she had said, softening. "Of course he's sympathetic, but he's too frightened of causing offence. He says the congregation is elderly and easily shocked. I've told him that we need a new congregation. If we had *your* sup-

41

port, it would give Edward confidence. We both have so much respect, you know, for your opinions.''

Then she began to discuss with him with great clarity and knowledge an article he had written in the church magazine, so he became seduced by her interest and learning, and when she went, he was never sure how things were between them. Perhaps she thinks I approve, he thought, and he would go to church the next week with some trepidation, expecting to find the dance group already active, or electric guitars, or a black gospel singer performing from the pulpit.

His first impulse when he saw Dorothea Cassidy's car was to pretend that he was out. Today he had more reason than usual to be afraid of her. With some shame he quickly drew the living-room curtains back together and stood in the stuffy half-light waiting for her to ring the doorbell. The waiting and the silence made his heart pound. He began to sweat. This isn't fair, he cried to himself. At my age I should be left in peace. What is the woman playing at? He crept to the kitchen in case she had gone to the back of the house, but there was no sign of her there. All the time he listened for the engine to start and the car to drive away. After ten minutes he decided that the tension of waiting was worse than facing her, so suddenly he threw the door open and called with all the courage he could muster.

''Dorothea! Where are you? Come in, my dear.''

But there was no reply and he was left feeling foolish and resentful, talking to himself in full view of everyone in the street. In the garden of Armstrong House next door, Clive Stringer, the teenage boy who worked there, stared at him, his mouth wide open, so he looked more gormless than ever. His presence confused Walter Tanner. He distrusted the boy and never knew what to say to him, but if Dorothea was around, he did not want her to catch him being impolite. He stood on the doorstep uncertainly and swore under his breath. Where was the woman?

One of the domestic staff was standing on a kitchen stool, halfheartedly polishing the windows of Armstrong House. Walter Tanner went to the boundary hedge and called to her. The woman carefully clambered down and cautiously approached him.

"Have you seen Mrs. Cassidy?" he asked. "Her car's here, but there's no sign of her."

Then, to his amazement, she backed away from him and began to cry, mopping her eyes with the hem of her overall.

"Man," she said. "Haven't you heard? Mrs. Cassidy's dead."

When Ramsay and Hunter arrived at Walter Tanner's house, he was eating his breakfast with a single man's economy of effort. The same plate was used for his egg and his toast and he stirred his tea with the handle of his knife. He had never married. He had thought, when he was a fervent young man, that he would join the priesthood, and none of the women he had met then had seemed possible vicar's wives. He had drifted into the family business, prompted by some sense of obligation, expecting it only to be a temporary measure. When his mother's health improved, when they could afford more reliable staff, he would leave, but neither condition was ever met and he suddenly found that he was too old either to train to be a priest or to marry.

The sound of the doorbell startled him and he piled the plate with its half-eaten food and the mug onto the draining board. Then he opened the door to the detectives, fumbling with the catch in his haste to let them in. He took them into the kitchen and had to open the curtains again. He shivered as he remembered with horror his attempt to hide from a dead woman. He felt terribly guilty, as if in desiring her absence he had been responsible for her death.

"Sit down," he said. "Sit down." Then he saw them looking around the room and saw it through their eyes—the furniture large and shabby, much of it remaining from when his parents had moved to the house when it was new in the thirties. The Tanners had been respected in the town then, they had mixed on almost equal terms with the gentry who came to the grand shop in Front Street. He had been a child and his mother had sent him to elocution lessons, insisting that if he grew up with a "common" accent, he would be no use to her in the shop. While his school friends went to the Sunday school in the Methodist chapel his mother took him to matins at St. Mary's. You get, she said, a better class of congregation there.

Now Walter Tanner felt as old and shabby as the furniture. A small, dumpy man with thinning grey hair and a sad moustache, he wore the same suit as he had always worn to the shop, before he retired and sold up. He was pleased he had changed from his slippers into black shoes. He felt vaguely that it would be disrespectful to mourn Dorothea in carpet slippers.

"You won't mind if I smoke," he said, stuttering over the last word. He felt in his trouser pocket and brought out a packet of cigarettes and a box of matches.

"This has all been a terrible shock."

"Yes," Ramsay said. "Of course. It must have been."

"When I saw the car, you see, I didn't know she was dead. I thought she had called for a visit. . . ." His voice tailed off. He held the cigarette lightly between his fingertips as if to show them that he was not a regular smoker, as if it were almost medicinal.

"Was it usual for Mrs. Cassidy to visit you without prior arrangement?" Ramsay asked.

"Oh, Dorothea never made appointments to see me," he said. "She turned up out of the blue when she felt like it." He realised, too late, how bad-tempered that sounded and added: "It was always a pleasure to see her, of course. Always a great pleasure."

44

'What is your position at St. Mary's?" Ramsay asked.

"I'm churchwarden," the man said. "And secretary of the parochial church council."

"I'm sorry," Ramsay said, "I thought Major Walker was churchwarden."

"He is. There are two of us. It's a lot of work, you know. More work than people realise. Major Walker lives out of the town and has a number of other commitments. They rely on me for day-to-day management."

He spoke with resentment and Ramsay thought it must be a long-standing grievance. The major, confident and articulate, would attract the attention and have the power, while Walter Tanner did all the work.

"Yes," Ramsay said slowly. "I see. Mr. Tanner, what exactly was the nature of your relationship with Mrs. Cassidy?"

He found it impossible to imagine that Dorothea would have chosen to come to this gloomy house to speak to this nondescript little man. Tanner looked up sharply and inhaled frantically on the cigarette.

"Relationship?" he said. "What do you mean?"

"You say that Mrs. Cassidy called to see you occasionally," Ramsay said. "Why did she do that?"

To make my life a misery, Tanner wanted to answer, but he paused and considered.

"She was young and enthusiastic," he said. "She had a lot of new ideas. I think she wore Edward out with them and then she would come to me."

"Did she expect you to help her?"

"No," Tanner said. "Not in any practical way. I think she just wanted my blessing."

"Did she get it?"

Tanner paused. He felt it impossible to explain to the policeman the ambiguity of his contact with Dorothea, his in-

45

ability to stop her in full flow, his lack of courage and conviction in front of her.

"No," he said at last, trying to sound firm. "I'm afraid I considered most of her schemes were unworkable and badly thought out. And she seemed to hold none of our traditions sacred."

"Was there antagonism between you about this?" Ramsay said. "Did she come here to make a fuss?"

He was still trying to discover what had drawn Dorothea to the man.

"No," Tanner said. "Of course not. We talked. That's all."

Ramsay decided to approach the thing from a different angle.

"It must have been rather a shock when Mr. Cassidy suddenly announced that he was intending to marry."

"Yes," Tanner said. "When he came to Otterbridge, he was a young widower. There were rumours later, of course, linking his name to some of the unattached ladies in the parish, but nothing came of it. It was a great surprise when he turned up suddenly with Dorothea."

"What do you mean?" Ramsay asked. "You must have known beforehand that he intended to marry."

"No," Tanner said, "Nobody knew. He took his annual holiday in the summer, and when he came back he was a married man. I understand they had only known each other for three months. He said that Dorothea wanted a quiet wedding, with just close family. No one from the parish was invited."

"I suppose his son must have known. . . ." Ramsay said.

"Oh, the boy was there," Tanner said dismissively.

"Why do you suppose that the vicar acted in such a hurry?"

"I don't know," Tanner said. "Perhaps he was afraid Dorothea would change her mind. Of course there was a

46

great deal of speculation about the secrecy and the haste. The whole affair rather damaged his reputation."

"Yet you would say that generally he's a popular man?"

"Yes," Tanner said, grudgingly. "Generally. When he first came to the parish, he had some outlandish ideas, but over the years we mellowed him."

Throughout Ramsay's conversation with Tanner, Hunter had remained standing. Now he began to move restlessly round the room. He felt trapped by the stuffy room and all these words. Why didn't Ramsay get to the point? He could stand it no more.

"When did you last see Mrs. Cassidy?" he asked abruptly, and the question so startled Tanner that he answered without realising the implication of the reply.

"Yesterday lunchtime," he said. "But not to speak to."

"She didn't come here?"

"Oh no," he said. "It was on the Ridgeway Estate. She was coming out of one of the houses there as I was walking past. I don't think she even saw me." He waited breathlessly for them to ask what he was doing on the Ridgeway Estate, but the question did not come.

"Did she have her car with her then?"

"Yes," Tanner said. "She was obviously in a hurry. She almost ran out of the house and drove away."

Hunter walked to the window and stared moodily out at the car, still parked on the drive. A colleague stood on the pavement, protecting it from the contaminating touches of passersby, waiting for the forensic team. Hunter would have preferred to be outside in the sunshine.

"Do you know the name of the street?" Ramsay asked. "It might be important."

Tanner thought. All he could remember was an overwhelming relief that Dorothea had not seen him. "It was one of those streets named after Victorian novelists," he said at last. "Eliot perhaps, or Hardy." Then, in a panic he added:

"I went there to visit one of our congregation who's been poorly." With the lie he almost felt faint.

"Could you give us a brief account of your movements yesterday afternoon?" Ramsay said.

"I got a bus from the Ridgeway back to town," Tanner said. "I went into the supermarket to do some shopping, then walked home through the park. There was a brass band playing as part of the festival and I stopped to listen. It was rather pleasant. I spent the rest of the afternoon and the evening in the house."

Ramsay had a sudden vision of his own life, after retirement. Would he spend his days in such a drab, friendless way, with the only excitement a brass band concert in the park? He could not stand it.

"Would you have noticed if the car was here when you went to bed last night?" he asked quietly.

Tanner stammered, "I don't know. Probably not. I drew the curtains at about ten. It wasn't here then. I was watching the television."

"But you would have heard the sound of the engine," Hunter said. "The drive's just outside the window. You would have seen the headlights even through the curtain."

"Perhaps," Tanner said unhappily.

"What time did you go to bed?"

"At about eleven," Tanner said. He wondered if he should tell them that he had been watching boxing on the television. He thought the detail might make his story more credible, but he was worried about what they would think of his taste in viewing. Dorothea had caught him watching a replay of a world title fight one afternoon and had said it was barbaric.

"You weren't disturbed at all in the night? No voices, unusual sounds?"

"No," he said. "But my bedroom's at the back of the house. I wouldn't have heard anything going on in the street."

"Do any of your neighbours keep late hours, work shifts?

It would be very helpful to find someone who saw the car arrive."

Tanner shook his head. "I'm sorry," he said. "I don't know. Armstrong House is next door. I suppose most of the residents there would go to bed rather early, but the warden might have been awake. I don't have a lot of contact with the rest of the street."

Ramsay stood up then and held out his hand to Tanner. The old man took it uncertainly. If there had just been the two of them, he thought, just he and the inspector, it might have been easier to explain. But the presence of the sergeant, so young and fit, so uncompromising, so like Dorothea in many ways, made it impossible. He walked with the policemen to the front door and saw them out of the house, then returned to the living room to watch them, peering like a prying old woman round the grey net curtains.

Ramsay stood on the drive and looked down the street. Tanner's garden was enclosed by a privet hedge, but the car must still be visible from one of the upstairs windows of Armstrong House. Perhaps some elderly insomniac had seen it driven there. The old people's flats were new, brick-built, and stood on a corner between the narrow street where Tanner lived and a much busier road. Previously the site had housed an old nursing home, which had closed down suddenly with the death of the owner and been allowed to become derelict before it was bought by the charitable organisation. Then it was demolished completely and the flats were built.

It seemed strange to Ramsay that Dorothea's car had been found so close to the place where she had an appointment. Had she made it to Armstrong House after all? But that made Aunt Annie and her friends suspects in a murder enquiry and what possible motive could they have?

Hunter was directing his attention to the car, taking care

49

not to touch anything. He took special interest in the back, which, because it was an estate, was exposed to view.

"There's a rug there," he said. "Do we know if that was here, in the car already?"

Ramsay shrugged.

"The keys are still in the ignition," Hunter said. He wanted to bring the inspector back to the concrete detail of the investigation. Nowadays crimes were solved by scientists, not by detectives asking endless questions and staring up at the sky. "No sign of the diary or the handbag, but they might be in the dash."

But still Ramsay looked down the street vaguely, as if somewhere behind the mock Tudor gables and stained glass porches he would find inspiration.

"How far is it to Prior's Park from here?" he asked suddenly.

Hunter looked up from the car.

"The little entrance is just at the end of the street," he said. "It's only a couple of minutes' walk away."

"Why here?" Ramsay demanded. "Why leave her car here? In the drive of someone who was known to her? Does that mean the murderer knew them both?"

That too, he thought, must be more than coincidence.

"Do you think the old boy had anything to do with it?" Hunter asked. The policeman turned toward the house and caught the eye of Tanner, who was looking out at them. Shamefacedly he let the net curtains drop and moved away from the window.

"No," Ramsay said. "Probably not. If he'd murdered Dorothea Cassidy, the last thing he'd do would be to bring her car here."

He felt suddenly that the solution to the case lay with Dorothea Cassidy. This wasn't a random attack on a pretty young woman in a park. It was more complicated, more purposeful than that. He felt that in the discussion with Walter Tanner

50

he had lost the clear image of the woman he had seen in the photographs. Tanner had disliked her and been frightened by her enthusiasm. Through his eyes the picture of Dorothea Cassidy had been distorted. In the vicarage Ramsay had felt that he had known her, and he wanted to recapture that intimacy. Unconsciously he echoed the thought of the boy who had found the body. What's wrong with me, he thought, that I'm attracted to a dead woman?

"Stay here," he said quietly to Hunter. "Wait until they come for the car, then organise a house-to-house of the street. I'm going to Armstrong House. They're a nebby lot. They might have seen something."

Annie Ramsay lived in Armstrong House and Annie Ramsay had known Dorothea well.

5

Clive Stringer carried the big television from the common room at Armstrong House to the repair van outside. The van's driver watched the feat of strength with amazement. He was standing on the pavement.

"Eh," he said. "I couldn't shift it. You're a strong lad."

He was a kind man and sensed that Clive Stringer received few compliments. The boy stared at him with distrust, his mouth open as if he had never got the hang of breathing through his nose. They were standing at the main entrance to the flats by the busy road and there was a lot of traffic noise.

"What are you doing working here then?" the electrician asked. It was more pleasant here outside than in his stuffy workshop and the boy's unnatural strength fascinated him. "Odd-job man, is it?"

"I was sent here," Clive Stringer said. "Community service for robbing houses."

His voice was jerky and excitable and the electrician felt a shudder of revulsion. He's one of those, he thought. Mental. His lift doesn't go all the way to the top. The boy came closer to him and reached out to touch his arm. Quickly, still smiling and nodding, the man climbed into his van. He drove away without saying anything more and Clive was left standing awkwardly in front of the flats, stammering, as if he had something important to say if only the man had waited long enough to listen.

Clive walked furtively round the flats toward the back entrance. From there he could see Dorothea Cassidy's car, and he stood staring at it, waiting for something to happen. When Walter Tanner emerged on the doorstep, calling out for Dorothea, he felt a desire to giggle, but he controlled himself. He thought that anyway there wasn't much to laugh about.

Clive knew he was in trouble. For as long as he could remember he had been in the sort of trouble that came from not understanding what was expected of him, from being different and awkward. That had been a vague unease, an awareness of unsuspected perils, that he had learned to cope with. But this was different. He knew quite definitely that he had done something wrong and that there was no one he could talk to who had the power to put it right.

I'll have to tell someone, he thought as he moved guiltily from the pavement into the cool of the building, but there was no one to confide in. His mother would not know what to do. He had tried relying on her and she had always let him down. Besides, now she could think of nothing else but the baby. Joss, his mother's boyfriend, was friendly enough when he was sober, but Clive never knew what to make of him and knew he could not be trusted. Those in authority over him— his probation officer, his social worker, the warden of Armstrong House—all had the power to put him in prison. They had made that quite clear on a number of occasions. This is your last chance, lad, they had said. Screw this up and you'll be away. For a long time they had frightened him with their descriptions of the youth custody establishment, and he knew they were all on the same side as the police. There had been times of crisis before, but then he had turned to Dorothea Cassidy, seeking her out in the vicarage, lurking in the street to wait until she came out. Now he knew that was impossible and Dorothea Cassidy would never help him again.

Emily Bowman sat by the window of her flat and looked out with irritation at Clive Stringer. What was the boy doing, loitering on the pavement with that vacant look on his face? Really they paid enough rent for the flats in Armstrong House at least to be entitled to staff with a modicum of intelligence. She sat back on the chair and felt the sting of burned skin on her shoulder as it touched the cushion. She was being unfair, she thought. Her irritation was the result of her tiredness and the late arrival of the ambulance. Clive Stringer had his uses and he had always been an easy target for her annoyance.

Emily Bowman was tempted for a moment to ring for the warden to ask if there was any news of the ambulance but knew it would be futile. There would be no news. She would have liked some tea, weak and fragrant with a sugary biscuit, but had no energy to get up and make her way to the kitchen. She looked round the room with a detached and calculating eye. Her furniture was solid, of good quality. She had chosen it herself. Her husband had been a decent man, but had a taste for the vulgar, and she had allowed him to make no decisions about the house. She moved in the chair and tried to make herself more comfortable as she dreamed of the old life, before Arthur died. They had lived in a bungalow in the best part of town. Arthur had never been promoted in the bank as she had hoped he might be, but he had given her security, a certain position. She had been chairman of the Townswomen's Guild for three years before she moved to Armstrong House. She closed her eyes and dozed, listening all the time for the ambulance, becoming slowly and more uncomfortably aware that she needed the lavatory.

I was strong then, she thought. Independent. Just like Dorothea Cassidy. I never thought it would come to this.

For five weeks Emily Bowman had spent every weekday morning in this state of anxious anticipating. By Friday she

54

was exhausted. First there was this wait for the ambulance, which was supposed to arrive at nine and was always late. Eventually it would come and the warden would help her outside, grasping her arm and patting her hand as if she needed reassurance when all she wanted was for the ordeal to be over. Then there was the bumpy and interminable drive round country lanes and suburban side streets while other patients were collected, the traffic jams at the lights on the Town Moor, the painfully slow crawl past badly parked cars in the hospital complex.

The arrival of the ambulance at the radiotherapy centre at Newcastle General Hospital was only the beginning of the waiting. As soon as she got to the centre she would go as fast as she could to the ladies' cloakroom to remove the undergarments of which the radiographers disapproved so strongly. "Wear loose clothes, Mrs. Bowman," they would say. "You'll be much more comfy without a bra. Look at the state of your skin. Have you used the powder regularly?" Mrs. Bowman did not tell them that the smell of the talcum powder they had given her to put on the affected area made her feel sick, or that she would *never* consider going without a bra, so the daily deception became necessary.

She would emerge from the toilet with her bra and vest in her handbag, like a naughty schoolgirl, mildly triumphant that she had not been caught, only to find that there was no need for the rush. There was always a different excuse for the delay. They said that the machine had been switched off for maintenance or that they were short-staffed. Everyone else seemed to take the waiting in their stride, even to enjoy the opportunity to compare the hours of travelling and side effects while they drank the dreadful WRVS tea. Emily hated it.

From the large waiting room with its pitiful attempts at homeliness—flower-patterned wallpaper, curtains, easy chairs—she was summoned eventually to a bench in the corridor. Here at least there was something to look at. She could see into the control room where radiographers in white uniforms worked the X-ray machines. One of the most complicated pieces of machinery had a brass plaque attached, saying that it had been bought by the Chester-Le-Street Ladies Circle. Why didn't they mind their own business, Emily sometimes thought bitterly, the ladies of Chester-Le-Street. If it weren't for their generosity, perhaps I wouldn't have to put up with this nonsense. Then she would be called in by one of the radiographers, who had the professional cheerfulness of a nursery nurse.

"Mrs. Bowman," she would say. "Strip to the waist, please."

As if I don't know that I have to take my clothes off, she thought, after a month of this. But she would go in meekly and suffer the indignity of being positioned on the table—sometimes by a man—and the lonely strangeness of the X-ray treatment itself, which only lasted a matter of minutes.

Then she had to wait for the ambulance to take her home.

A young woman doctor had broken the news to her that she had cancer. She had been very gentle, very sympathetic.

"Sit down, Mrs. Bowman," she had said. "Don't hold in your feelings. Cry if you want to. It's bound to be a shock."

But Mrs. Bowman had not felt like crying. The first sensation had been of exhilaration. This is it then, she had thought. It's all over, but I've had a good life. She had one son, but he had lived for years in New Zealand. No one would miss her. She had never been one for taking risks and this was the most exciting thing that had ever happened to her. There was something dramatic about being incurably ill and she had expected a sudden change in her condition, then the final adventure of death. She had not expected the fuss, the tedium, and the discomfort of this treatment. It seemed to her a complete waste of time. Even the young doctor had the decency to admit that it had little chance of succeeding.

Yet there seemed no way of stopping the process. Emily felt powerless in front of their humanity, their determination to do all they could to save her.

Stop! she wanted to say as she lay on the table and the machine above her head clicked and buzzed. Leave me alone. Really. I've had a good life and I'm ready to go now.

But she was so worn down by the waiting and the WRVS tea that when she finally got to the treatment room, she did not have the courage or the energy to say anything.

She must have fallen asleep in her chair by the window and she woke, quite suddenly, shivering, knowing that she had had a bad dream but unable to remember it. The sun was full on her face and very hot. The skin on her shoulder was burning.

"Let the air to your body," the radiographers would say. "Take your clothes off for at least an hour every day."

Emily Bowman breathed deeply, still disturbed by the dream, then pursed her lips. If they thought she would sit naked in her flat where any of the other residents might come in and see her, they were very much mistaken. Yet she could feel the sun irritating her burnt skin and knew she would have to move. Besides, by now her bladder was full and she would have to go to the bathroom. It was one of her nightmares that she would have to ask the ambulance driver to stop on the way to the hospital. She stood up slowly and walked with difficulty to the bathroom. She was on her way back to the chair when Annie Ramsay burst into the room.

"This is my flat," Emily snapped. "I'd be grateful if you had the courtesy to knock."

She flushed with anger and the release of the tension caused by the waiting. One of the compensations of her illness was that she no longer cared what people thought of her. She was excused rudeness. She could say exactly what she chose.

Annie Ramsay was unperturbed by the hostility. Since Emily's arrival at the Armstrong House, she had taken it upon herself to make the woman feel welcome, bringing homemade cakes and invitations to the afternoon bingo sessions with each visit. Emily Bowman had reacted to the attention at first with haughty politeness and later with more direct requests to be left alone. Annie Ramsay seemed not to hear or to understand.

"It's no trouble, man," she would say, settling into Emily's own easy chair with her knitting. "We're neighbours and both on our own. It's a pleasure to have someone to chat to."

But we have nothing in common, Emily wanted to say. My husband worked in a bank and yours down the pit. You've probably never read a book in your life and the very idea of bingo makes me want to scream. But as the cancer and the radiotherapy sapped all her energy she resisted less. She even found some relief in Annie Ramsay's visits. She talked so much that Emily was required to make no contribution to the conversation. There was something relaxing about Annie's gossip. It was like easy melodic popular music. Her irritability at these regular interruptions had become meaningless and ritual.

Annie Ramsay was a small woman, very tough and thin with stringy arms. All her clothes seemed too big for her. Her sparse hair was permed every month into tight curls.

"We mustn't let ourselves go," she would say to Emily, "just because we're on our own."

At the Armstrong House socials she would make a beeline for the unattached men and flirt with them. Sometimes Emily suspected that she had been drinking.

Now Annie seemed strangely subdued. Emily thought she had been crying.

"I've some news," Annie said, and even in her sadness she found it impossible not to make a drama of the situation, so she added: "You'd best sit down. I'll not take the risk of telling you while your standing. The shock might have you over."

Although it was still in full sunlight, Emily returned to the chair by the window, because from there she had a view of the main street and would see the ambulance arriving.

"What is this all about?" she said, but her eyes were still on the traffic outside. When she turned back to the room, Annie was crying again.

"Come on," Emily said, more kindly. "It can't be as bad as all that."

"It's Dorothea Cassidy," Annie said in a whisper. "She's dead."

At first she could not tell if the woman had heard her. There was no reaction and that was disappointing. Everyone else in the place had expressed shock, horror, and a desire for all the details. Emily Bowman had been a regular at St. Mary's until her illness meant she couldn't get out. She knew Dorothea Cassidy as well as any of them, and Annie thought it would have been more fitting to show some grief.

"Did you hear?" Annie said more loudly. "Dorothea Cassidy is dead."

"I heard," Emily said. She shivered again as she had done when waking from the dream. She was not surprised. I wish it had been me, she thought. It should have been me.

"It was me that raised the alarm," Annie Ramsay said. She could not keep the self-importance from her voice. "She was coming to talk to the residents' association about her work in Africa. She had slides, you know, of all the poor little black babies. When she didn't turn up, I knew something was wrong. I felt it in my bones. That's why I phoned our Stephen. I thought he'd know what to do."

Emily Bowman dragged her eyes away from the street below her.

"What happened?" she demanded. "How did she die?"

Annie Ramsay had been waiting for the opportunity and leaned forward.

"She was murdered," she said. "Strangled to death. Two boys found her in Prior's Park early this morning."

Emily shut her eyes, then opened them and fixed Annie with a fierce stare.

"How do you know all this?" she said. "Have you spoken to your nephew about it?"

"No," Annie answered with some regret. "I phoned the station earlier but they said he was busy. I heard it on Radio Newcastle. The police are asking for anyone who saw her yesterday to come forward."

Emily moved uncomfortably in her chair.

"I saw her yesterday," she said carelessly, though she must have been aware of the excitement it would cause Annie. "She was here yesterday afternoon. She came to visit me."

At that moment the warden knocked on the door and said that Inspector Ramsay was downstairs and would like to speak to Annie.

Annie Ramsay took her nephew to her own flat. She did not want Emily Bowman to steal her glory and decided she would save the information that Dorothea Cassidy had been in Armstrong House the afternoon before until the end of the conversation. She walked beside him down the wide corridor, holding on to his arm, hoping all her friends would see her. In her flat she sat him in her favourite chair and made him tea, ignoring his insistence that he was in a hurry.

"Now, pet," she said. "How can I help you?" She thought it the most natural thing in the world that he should come to her for help.

"I want you to tell me about Dorothea Cassidy." he said. "I know you go to St. Mary's. What was she like?"

"She was a treasure," Annie Ramsay said. "Man, we were lucky to have her there. She brought the whole place to life. And the laughs we had!"

"In what way did she bring the place to life?"

"She was all questions. She made us think. When you're old like us, you take it all for granted. We were brought up to go to church—not like the bairns these days—and for some of us it has no more meaning than a trip to the co-op. Then she came and the talks we had. . . ."

She wiped her eyes.

"There must have been some opposition," he said, "if she began to challenge the old ways of doing things."

"Ah well," she said. "You get stick-in-the-muds everywhere."

"What about Walter Tanner?" he asked. "Is he a stick-in-the-mud?"

"Man," she said. "He's the biggest stick-in-the-mud in the world."

"Dorothea's car was found in his drive this morning," he said.

The gem of information cheered her. "But that's only next door."

"That's why I'm here. Did you see anything last night?"

"Why no. If I'd seen it last night, I'd have told you."

"Would you have noticed it?"

She paused, considering. "No," she said. "Probably not. My flat's at the front, you see. You canna see Tanner's house from here."

"And you didn't go out last night?"

"No," she said, and smiled. "I wouldn't have minded going to the fair, but I was worried about Dorothea. And I couldn't find anyone to take me." She looked at Ramsay intently. "Tanner wouldn't have killed her," she said. "They might have had their differences, but there's no violence in him. He's too boring for that and he's not a bad man."

"What did he do before he retired?" Ramsay asked.

"His family had that posh grocer's in Front Street. You must have seen him in there."

Ramsay shook his head, but he remembered that his ex-wife, Diana, had shopped at Tanner's. "I wouldn't go anywhere else," she would say to her friends. "It's the only place in Northumberland where you can get a decent piece of Brie. And real old-fashioned service."

"What about Edward Cassidy?" Ramsay asked. "Whose side did he take in all this?"

"Edward Cassidy never took a side in his life. Not since he moved to Otterbridge at any rate. He's spent so much time sitting on the fence you'd think he'd have a hole in his pants." She stopped suddenly, aware that Ramsay was impatient and wanting to move on.

"I've some news for you," she said. "Something I think will help. Mrs. Cassidy was here yesterday afternoon."

"Did you see her?"

"No," she said regretfully. "I must have been at the bingo. But I can introduce you to someone who did. Her name's Emily Bowman. She's very poorly." She whispered the word. "Mrs. Cassidy came to visit her regularly because she couldn't make it to church. Shall I take you to meet her?"

But Ramsay was not prepared to give the time to another old lady. It was interesting, of course, but visiting the sick was a traditional occupation for a vicar's wife and he was convinced that in the end it would be Dorothea's other activities which would lead to her murderer. He wanted to find out about the case conference.

"I'll send Hunter, my sergeant, along. He's doing house-to-house enquiries in the street." He smiled at her. "You'll like him," he said. "He's a good-looking chap."

Then he left, because what motive could an old lady who was dying of cancer have for murder?

Clive Stringer was in the garden picking up the litter that had blown there from the street when the policeman arrived at the flats. The policeman was in plain clothes, but Clive's experience of the police went back to early childhood. There

62

was something about the way they stood, their confidence, the way they looked about them which gave them away. He continued to pick up the litter, moving with slow, stooped movements over the grass, filling the black plastic sack which he carried in one hand. He was wearing gloves. The warden always insisted that he should wear gloves when he was working with the rubbish. She was afraid that he would catch germs. Yet every time he put a scrap of paper or a can into the sack he glanced sideways, so he saw the tall policeman walk away from Dorothea's car and into the front door of the Armstrong House.

That's it, he thought. They know. It never occurred to him that there was no way they *could* know. He continued to work, but when the old man from next door came out of his house, he dropped the plastic sack and put the gloves in his pocket.

Distracted for a moment from his worry, he grinned maliciously and followed Walter Tanner up the street.

In the small house Walter Tanner had felt trapped. There were things he needed to do, but he felt he could not leave while Hunter and the police constable stood outside on the pavement. They might ask where he was going. He began to devise some fictitious explanation but felt suddenly ashamed that he could have considered such deceit. He hadn't sunk, he hoped, to lying. It was unnecessary. He went to the kitchen and began to wash up his breakfast dishes. Usually he left the plates on the draining board, but today, because he wanted to delay for as long as possible a decision about going out, he dried them on a threadbare tea towel and put them away. By the time he had hung the tea towel to dry on the oven door and returned to the living room, the car had disappeared from the drive and Hunter and the constable were on the other side of the road, knocking at doors, talking to neighbours. Even if they saw him leave the house, Tanner thought,

63

there was nothing they could do to stop him. He had not, after all, been placed under some sort of house arrest. This anxiety was ridiculous.

He waited until Hunter was right at the end of the street before leaving the house. Hunter was the one who frightened him. He would not listen to excuses or explanations. There would be no shades of grey with Hunter. Out in the street Tanner felt very exposed. He hurried, making his short legs walk very fast. He turned once and saw the half-wit from Armstrong House lurching up the street behind him.

What's the matter with the boy? he thought. Why is he persecuting me like this?

He walked faster until he was almost running, but when he caught the bus toward the Ridgeway Estate, Clive Stringer followed him and sat in the seat across the aisle from him, grinning all the time.

6

The social services office for north Otterbridge was only a street away from Armstrong House and it backed onto the park. Ramsay worried about whether the geographical closeness had any significance but came to no conclusion. The street was wider than that where Walter Tanner lived and the houses were larger. There were smooth green lawns and trees to ensure privacy. The only indication that the social services were housed in the building was a discreet sign by the gate and a car park at the end of the drive. Next door there was an exclusive private nursery, and as Ramsay left his car he heard the fluting sound of a Joyce Grenfell nursery nurse calling to her charges. He wondered what the social workers' clients who lived on the Ridgeway Estate thought of these surroundings. It would be like walking into another world.

The senior social worker who had worked most closely with Dorothea Cassidy was called Hilary Masters. Ramsay had never met her, though Hunter had come across her when he was investigating a series of school arsons, and she had been for a while the subject of his canteen gossip. He had nicknamed her the Snow Queen.

"Talk about icy," he had said. "Man, she'd freeze your

balls off." He had spoken with regret. "She's a beauty, mind."

"Perhaps," Ramsay had said, "she's just discriminating."

"Aye, well. Perhaps you're right. She might go for your type. But I like my women to have a bit of life in them, all the same. There's something weird about that one."

Because of that exchange, Ramsay felt Hilary Masters was worthy of admiration—he had never trusted Hunter's judgement—and as he waited in the reception room he was nervous, and at the same time prepared to be disappointed.

He was shown into a large, airy office and saw a tall woman in her thirties. She was single, obviously independent, and Ramsay thought she would be ambitious. She was dressed in a cotton skirt and blouse in swirling pastel colours which did not suit her. Her legs were very long and her feet rather big. Yet she was, as Hunter had said, a beauty. Her face was startling—oval, flawless, and perfectly symmetrical. She sat behind her desk and stared at him with calm grey eyes.

The police station had been in touch with her and she was expecting him.

"Inspector Ramsay," she said. "How can I help you?"

He felt ill at ease with her. Partly it was her perfect face and her air of competence, but he felt, too, that she was magically perceptive. She seemed to know his weakness just by looking at him. But he was not disappointed by her.

"I'm investigating the murder of Dorothea Cassidy," he said. "I understand that she was here for a case conference yesterday."

She paused, as if wondering if it were against her principles even to tell him that.

"Yes," she said at last. "She was here yesterday."

"Can you tell me what the conference was about?"

She frowned. "Is it relevant to your investigation?"

"It might be. We're trying to trace Mrs. Cassidy's movements yesterday. She was seen at lunchtime on the Ridgeway Estate. Perhaps you could tell me who she had gone to visit there."

Hilary Masters sat quite still.

"A woman called Stringer," she said. "Theresa Stringer."

"Was she the subject of the case conference?"

"No," she said reluctantly. "It was her daughter, Beverley. We had to decide whether or not she should be taken into care."

"What decision did you come to?"

"We decided that we would go for a place-of-safety order."

"What does that mean?"

She looked at him as if offended by his ignorance. "It meant that we thought she would be at risk if she were left at home."

He wondered if the measured, uninformative answers were designed to provoke him to anger. Why was she so hostile? Did she dislike him personally or all men in authority? He recognised her prickly defensiveness as part of himself.

"What sort of risk was she in?" he asked evenly. "Neglect, sexual abuse, physical abuse."

"It was a complicated situation," she said. "We were worried about the influence of her mother's boyfriend. His name's Corkhill. Joss Corkhill."

Her apparent inability to give a direct answer frustrated him, but he kept his patience.

"Perhaps you could tell me all about the case," he said carefully, "and about how Dorothea Cassidy came to be involved. I understand that you have ethics to consider, but you can understand how important it is."

She paused and shrugged.

"We've been involved in the Stringer family for a long time," she said. "Theresa was a difficult child, not very

67

bright, rather disturbed. She went to a number of special schools. Her parents were elderly. They did their best for her, but when she left school, they couldn't cope and threw her out. She worked for a while as a chambermaid in a hotel in the Midlands, then turned up here again, homeless and pregnant.''

''And Beverley was born?''

''No,'' she said. ''Not then. I explained that Theresa has been known to the department for a long time. The baby was a boy. She called him Clive. Now he's sixteen.''

''Did Theresa cope with bringing up the child by herself?''

Hilary Masters shrugged. ''She tried her best,'' she said. ''She was very fond of him. We gave her all the support we could. The council found her a hard-to-let house on the Ridgeway—it was easier to get a council house sixteen years ago. We've had a social worker visiting the family since that time. Clive was put on the ''at risk'' register when he was born, not because we thought Theresa meant to harm him but because she could be careless, thoughtless about his safety. She let him wander about the estate when he was a very young child. It was hardly surprising that he first got into trouble when he was nine.''

''What sort of trouble?'' Ramsay was unsure how much value this information could have for the murder investigation, but he had asked Miss Masters to tell him about the family.

''I'm surprised you've not heard of him,'' she said, ''though perhaps you've more important things to deal with than a petty thief. . . .'' He thought she might be sneering at him, but when he looked at her, she was quite serious. ''Clive has been in the juvenile court on numerous occasions,'' she said. ''Mostly for vehicle-related offences—taking and driving away and the theft of car radios. He seems to have an obsession about cars.''

''Is he still at school?'' Ramsay asked.

She shook her head. "He left officially at Christmas, but he hasn't attended regularly for a couple of years. He's always had problems at school. He struggled even in the remedial stream. A different parent might have pushed for him to have special help, but Theresa had experienced the stigma of going to a special school and didn't want that for her son."

"So what is he doing now? YTS?"

"No," she said. "He started on a scheme in a garage in town but it never came to anything. I don't know exactly what happened. He said the boss picked on him, but I doubt it he was very reliable. Then he appeared in court again and that seemed to be the final straw. He got the sack about three months ago."

She began to straighten a pile of printed forms in front of her. Ramsay wondered if she had finished her story, but it seemed she was just starting to come to the point. She hesitated, still unsure how much to give away.

"That was when Dorothea Cassidy took him on," she said. "She was a qualified social worker, you know, very experienced, and sometimes she did some voluntary work for us, on difficult cases that need more time than most field workers have."

Ramsay said nothing.

"We had our differences," the woman went on. "I found Dorothea's approach disturbing, risky. She was too involved, unprofessional. But she seemed to work wonders with Clive Stringer. She even persuaded him to go to church with her." This time there *was* a sneer in her voice.

Still, Ramsay remained intently silent and she continued:

"When Clive last appeared in court, Dorothea went and spoke up for him. He was expecting youth custody—we all thought that this time he would definitely go away—but she persuaded the magistrates to consider another supervision order. She told them that Clive had agreed to do some community service. She said it would be a fitting reparation for him to give something back to the more frail and vulnerable residents of the town.''

She smiled, and for the first time Ramsay thought she might have a sense of humour. ''Dorothea was magnificent in court,'' she said. ''There wasn't a dry eye in the house. She was terribly effective at that kind of thing.''

''What sort of community service?'' Ramsay asked.

''Oh,'' Hilary said, ''she had persuaded the warden of Armstrong House to let him work there.''

Ramsay looked up sharply.

''Was he working at Armstrong House yesterday?''

She seemed surprised by his sudden interest. ''I expect so,'' she said. ''He worked there most days. Why?''

''It appears that Dorothea was there visiting a sick old lady yesterday afternoon,'' Ramsay said, ''and she was due to speak to the residents' association in the evening. Then her car was found this morning outside a house next door to the old people's flats. It all seems rather too much of a coincidence.''

''You can't think that Clive Stringer had anything to do with her murder,'' Hilary said. ''He's a bit simple, but there's no history of violence. And he adored her. I was worried that he had become too dependent on her. He'll need special help now, to come to terms with her death.''

There was a knock on the door and a young social worker came in. He blushed awkwardly and held out a sheet of typed paper.

''Sorry to disturb you,'' he said. ''This is the social report you wanted, Hilary.''

She was obviously irritated by the interruption and took the report without a word. He backed his way out of the room, stepping on his lace and stumbling. Ramsay was horrified that such an ineffective boy should have the power to commit a client to mental hospital or a child into care. He waited until the social worker had shut the door behind him, then continued.

"Perhaps you could give me the background to yesterday's case conference. You said there was a second child. Was Corkhill the father?"

"No," she said. "He's come onto the scene fairly recently. Theresa would never tell us the identity of Beverley's father. She might not have known it. I'd always presumed that the pregnancy was the result of a casual relationship."

"If, as you say, she's irresponsible, isn't it surprising that there weren't more children?"

"There was another child," Hilary said. "A daughter, Nicola. She died suddenly when she was six months old. It was a typical cot death. Clive was three or four at the time. Theresa was dreadfully upset. I think it shocked her into being more careful for a while."

"Were there any suspicious circumstances surrounding Nicola's death?" Ramsay asked.

Hilary Masters shook her head. "No more than with any cot death," she said. "The police accepted that it was accidental."

"How old is Beverley?"

"Two and a half. We were very pleased with the way that Theresa was coping until Corkhill moved in with her."

"When was that?"

"Just after Christmas." She paused. "Corkhill's rather a romantic figure. Quite unreliable, but I can understand why Theresa was taken in by him. He even charmed Dorothea, though she knew he had an extensive record. He was born in Liverpool and has moved around a lot. Not only here, but in Ireland and the States. It's hard to imagine, though, how he made the arrangements or got enough money for his travels. He's probably alcoholic—certainly he drinks very heavily. I gather that there was a brief marriage when he was very young, but this is probably the longest he's settled anywhere since he left home as a teenager. He's always had temporary labouring jobs then moved on. His longest period of employment was with one of those tacky fairgrounds that move round the country. Apparently he came to the northeast to work on one of those rides at the Town Moor Hoppings and stayed on. I'm not sure where he met Theresa.''

"What's he been done for?'' Ramsay asked. The name was unfamiliar.

"Mostly drunk and disorderly. Some petty theft. And there was one charge of assault after a fight in a bar in Newcastle.''

"Is he working now?''

"He's been unemployed since he moved in with Theresa, but this week he's been helping with the fair on the abbey meadow. He met up again with some old contacts. That's partly why we're so concerned.''

"I don't understand,'' Ramsay said.

"There was some suspicious bruising on Beverley's body,'' Hilary Masters said. "When he's drunk, Joss is unpredictable, moody. We think it's possible that he hit her.''

"And on those grounds you took her into care?''

He realised, too late, that he sounded critical. She became embarrassed, defensive.

"This is an impossible job, Inspector,'' she said. "When I was a student, one of the social workers in the team where I was training was called before a public enquiry after the death of a child she was supervising. I'll never forget it. The press camped out in her garden and followed her wherever she went. No one could withstand that sort of pressure and in the end she had a nervous breakdown.''

"I'm sorry,'' he said. He wanted to tell her that he understood, that he, too, had made a mistake which had ended in tragedy. "I wasn't trying to tell you how to do your job.''

She shrugged. "Why not?'' she said. "Everyone else does.'' Then she smiled. "I'm sorry,'' she said. "Paranoia goes with the work.'' She paused. "You're right, of course.

In normal circumstances we wouldn't take a child into care without stronger grounds. But in this case the circumstances were exceptional. I've explained that Joss had renewed his contacts with his friends on the fairground. The day before yesterday he and Theresa suddenly announced that they intended to leave Otterbridge and become travellers themselves, taking Beverley with them. And Clive, if he wanted to go. Practical problems like where they would live or whether Joss could make enough money to keep them seem not to have occurred to them. They're like children. It's all a game."

"So that precipitated the decision about taking the girl into care?"

"Of course. This is the last day of the festival. Tomorrow the fair will pack up and leave. We couldn't risk the family disappearing." She hesitated. "I suppose I hoped it would shock Theresa to her senses. I suspect that Joss has got itchy feet and wants to be off. She won't let him go."

"When did you suspect that Corkhill was ill-treating Beverly?"

The defensiveness returned. "We had no statutory involvement with the family," Hilary Masters said. "Only through Clive. Beverley was going to nursery regularly and seemed to be thriving."

"Who alerted you to what was going on?" Ramsay asked. Then it became obvious. "Was it Dorothea Cassidy?"

Perhaps that explained some of the social worker's hostility toward the vicar's wife. An amateur had succeeded where she had failed. He could understand how Hilary must feel.

Hilary Masters nodded.

"As I explained, Clive started going to church. Dorothea ran a youth club there and he started going to that. Then she persuaded him to go to the service on Sunday, too. I wasn't very happy about it. What right had she to impose her beliefs on an impressionable boy? I got his social worker, Mike

Peacock, to talk to him about it once. He told him that it wasn't part of his supervision order and he didn't have to go if he didn't want to.''

"What did he say?''

She shrugged. "That he enjoyed it. I think he had a teen-age crush on Dorothea. Not many people have been kind to him. After a few weeks he started taking Beverley to Sunday school. I suppose Theresa was glad to be rid of her for an hour, but it was probably Dorothea's idea.''

"And she thought Beverley was being ill-treated?''

Hilary Masters nodded.

"At first she noticed a change of personality. Beverley had always been a bright, outgoing child. She seemed unnaturally withdrawn and listless. Then she found the bruises. As I've explained, she was an experienced social worker. She realised that it was unlikely that they had been caused accidentally.''

"Did the child tell you that Corkhill had hit her?''

"No," Hilary said. "She refused to talk about it. But that's not unusual in child-abuse cases.''

"But you were convinced that Corkhill was the culprit?''

"Oh yes," Hilary said. "We were all convinced of that. When he was sober, he was helpful, courteous, but when he had been drinking, he had a foul temper. He's given Theresa a black eye after a row.''

"Where's the little girl now?''

"With foster parents.''

There was a silence. Ramsay thought there was something else which the social worker had failed to tell him.

"Can you tell me what happened at the case conference yesterday?'' he said. "What position did Dorothea Cassidy take?''

He thought at first Hilary would refuse to reply, but she answered reluctantly.

"She believed we should leave Beverley at home,'' she

said. "She liked Joss Corkhill. I think, despite her experience, she allowed herself to be manipulated. And she was extremely idealistic. There was a lot of talk yesterday at the case conference about a child being better off with its mother. She thought she could persuade Theresa to stay in Otterbridge."

"But you didn't?"

"I wasn't prepared to take the risk. In the past Theresa has never been susceptible to rational persuasion. I said that if Joss Corkhill left the town with the fair and Theresa stayed at home, then of course there would no longer be any grounds to keep Beverley in care. Dorothea was going to Theresa's house yesterday to talk to her about it."

"How did Mrs. Cassidy seem at the case conference?" Ramsay asked. "She wasn't upset or unusually preoccupied?"

"No," Hilary said. "She was enthusiastic, optimistic. Quite normal."

"Did you notice if she had a sticking plaster on her wrist?" Ramsay asked. "We think she may have cut herself at some point during the day."

If Hilary was surprised by the question, she gave no indication.

"No," she said. "I'm sure she didn't."

"What was the result of her meeting with Theresa after the case conference?" he asked.

"I don't know," Hilary said. "And that's surprising. I would have expected Dorothea to call in or to phone me after she'd spoken to Theresa. I'll be sending her social worker there this morning. We have to know what Theresa intends to do."

"Could I go with your social worker?" Ramsay asked. "I have to talk to Miss Stringer about Dorothea's visit yesterday. She might find it easier to talk to me if I'm with someone she knows."

Hilary Masters stood up.

"If you feel you need my staff's protection," she said icily, "I'm sure we can come to some arrangement."

The sarcasm surprised him. He had thought that they had reached some understanding. He felt a wave of sympathy for her and thought she must be as lonely as he was.

"Thank you for your time and your help," he said. He wanted to show her that he admired her, that he realised she was good at her job. "I must congratulate you. You have a very detailed knowledge of what must be only one of hundreds of cases your staff are supervising."

She looked at him, unsure whether or not he was mocking her, but when she saw it was meant as a compliment, she answered seriously.

"I told you, Inspector. It's never a trivial matter to take a child into care, no matter what the tabloid papers say. I always want to be sure of my facts. Besides, I know the family well. Before I was made a senior, I was the Stringers' social worker. It was the first case I took on when I arrived here, newly qualified. You might say that Theresa and I have grown up together."

He did not know what to say and left the office nervously, surprised that he cared so much what impression Hilary Masters had gained of him.

7

*A*t the last minute Hilary Masters decided to visit the Stringer family herself. Ramsay decided that she was what his ex-wife Diana would have called a control freak. She was afraid that the young social worker who had directly supervised the family would let down her team, that his attitude would reflect badly on her. She preferred to be in control of situations. He could understand the attitude. Diana had called him a control freak, too.

"We'll take my car," she said, taking charge again. "I know where we're going. It'll be quicker."

He said nothing and followed her downstairs, waited while she gave instructions to the receptionist, then followed her outside. It was nearly midday and very hot. The car seat burned through the back of his shirt, and even with both windows open he began to sweat. Hilary Masters remained cool and frostily pale. She drove well with a minimum of effort. They went down Armstrong Street past the old people's flats. Hunter was still knocking at doors and Ramsay was torn for a moment. Perhaps, after all, he should speak to the old lady who had seen Dorothea in the afternoon. But he did not want Hilary Masters to think him indecisive and he said nothing.

Hunter was continuing the thankless task of looking for a

witness who might have seen Dorothea Cassidy's car being driven onto Tanner's drive. Most of the residents seemed elderly, deaf. It was so rowdy during festival week, they said. They preferred to be in their beds.

He came to a house where he thought the residents must have recently moved in. The grass in the front garden was long and an estate agent's board had been pulled out and lay against the wall. Through the living-room window he could see evidence of renovation. There was little furniture. The upstairs curtains were still drawn. Hunter rang the bell. There was no reply and he rang it again and banged on the door with his fist. Inside, there was a muffled thud and an angry voice demanding to know what the hell was going on. He rang the bell again and there were footsteps on the stairs. The door opened.

It was obvious to Hunter that the young man inside had a hangover. He recognised the symptoms. He would have to be treated gently.

"I'm sorry to disturb you, sir," he said quietly. "I'm from Northumbria police. Perhaps I could come in."

And the young man, wrapped only in a bathrobe, slow-witted with the drink, could do nothing to stop him.

"What's the time?" he demanded as Hunter walked straight through to the kitchen and put on the kettle for tea.

"Eleven o'clock," said Hunter.

"Bloody hell," he said. "I'm late for work."

"That's all right," Hunter said. "You can tell your employer you were helping the police in a murder enquiry. They can phone me if there's any problem. Do you keep the tea in here?"

"Murder?" the young man said. "What murder?"

Hunter sat him down and made sure that he was listening properly, then explained about the murder of Dorothea Cassidy.

"Her car was found this morning parked in a drive on the

other side of the road," he said. "We're looking for witnesses who might have seen it driven there. Where were you yesterday evening?"

"In a pub," the man said. "In several pubs." He moaned. "I'm a morris man." Then, as Hunter seemed not to understand, "You know, morris dancing. We were performing as part of the festival."

"What time did you get home?" Hunter regarded the man suspiciously. He looked more like a rugby player than a morris dancer. It seemed a strange activity for a grown man.

The man shook his head painfully. "I don't know," he said. "Late. Well after midnight. I walked back."

"Was anyone about in the street?"

"No. I don't think so. They go to bed very early round here." He stood up and poured himself a glass of water. "There was the drunk. . . ."

"What drunk?"

"I suppose he was drunk. He nearly knocked me off the pavement."

"What sort of car was he driving?"

"It was one of those Morris thousand estates. My mam and dad had one when I was a kid."

"Are you sure the driver was a man?" Hunter asked.

"I'm not sure of anything. I was pissed. The car came up the road toward me. The road was clear but it swerved, so two of the wheels were on the pavement. I jumped clear and it drove off."

"Where did it go then?"

"I don't know. I wasn't interested. I just wanted to get home to my bed." He paused. "It might have stopped further down the street," he said, "but I can't really remember."

"Tell me what the driver looked like," Hunter said.

"I don't know. I didn't see. There are only a couple of

79

street lamps along here and his headlights dazzled me. It could have been a woman. It could have been anyone.''

It was all he could say. Hunter tried to bully more information out of him, but in the end he gave up. No one else in the street had seen or heard anything.

Annie Ramsay had been planning to visit the St. Mary's coffee morning, but after the inspector's visit she decided she would not go. There would have been some pleasure in explaining that it had been she who had first alerted the police to investigate Dorothea's disappearance, but she was afraid of missing further excitement. Besides, by now the event would almost be over and she would be roped in to clear up.

Although she usually disliked sloppy eating, she made a sandwich for an early lunch and ate it from a tray on her knees, sitting in an easy chair pulled up close to the window. From there she could see the main entrance of Armstrong House and she saw Hunter appear suddenly below her. She recognised him—Ramsay had brought him to a couple of the weekly tea parties for moral support. Without emptying her mouth, she set the tray on the windowsill and jumped to her feet, afraid that Hunter might find Emily Bowman's room without her assistance. In the corridor she paused, uncertain whether she should take the lift or the stairs to the ground floor. Usually she took the lift, but surely a fit young man like Hunter would want to walk and she was afraid of missing him. She grasped the bannister firmly and with determination began the descent to the ground floor.

Halfway down she realised she had made the right decision. She heard light young footsteps and the warden calling up to him:

''Mrs. Bowman is the number thirteen. The second on the left.''

She turned a corner and he was there, sprinting up the stairs towards her, so quickly that she was afraid he would pass her before she could catch her breath to speak.

"Mr. Hunter," she gasped. "It *is* Mr. Hunter." He stopped and she held out her hand to him and smiled. "You know my nephew," she said. "I don't expect you recognise me. It's Annie Ramsay."

He was balanced on his back leg with his front foot on the next step. He smiled at her. He was good with old ladies. He just had to turn on the charm and they adored him.

"I'm glad I caught you," Annie Ramsay went on. "I wanted to warn you about Emily. . . ." She paused, still wheezing from her hurried flight from her room. "She's very poorly." There was another hesitation, then she mouthed noiselessly, "Cancer. She is riddled with it."

In her strategy to be present at the interview, it was the most effective thing she could have said. Hunter was terrified by illness. He could face road accidents without squeamishness, and once when an ear was severed from a thug's head in a pub brawl, he had picked it up and taken it to the ambulance man in case it might be reattached. But disease was different. It struck at random, without provocation. It robbed a person of everything Hunter considered important.

Annie Ramsay must have recognised his unease because she pressed home her point.

"She has to go to the General every day for X-ray treatment," she said. "Poor thing. I don't know how she puts up with it."

Hunter hated hospitals. He said nothing.

"I was wondering," Annie said, as if she were doing him the biggest favour in the world. "I was wondering if you'd like me to be there with you. When you talk to her. Just in case, you know . . ."

He nodded gratefully, and in triumph Annie climbed the stairs again to Emily's room.

It was Annie who tapped on the door and Annie who went in first.

"Emily dear," she said. "There's a policeman to see you.

81

It's all right. It's Sergeant Hunter. He's a friend of my nephew's. He wants to talk to you because Dorothea came to visit you yesterday. They're trying to trace her movements.''

Emily Bowman was sitting in the same chair. She was still waiting for the ambulance. It gets later every day, she thought. Goodness knows what time it turned up yesterday. The others looked at her. They thought she had been dozing, unaware of the obsessive attention turned on the street. Once she had been a large, powerfully built woman. Now she seemed all bone, hard and fleshless, with knotted knuckles resting on a bony lap.

"Emily dear," Annie said again. "I don't believe you've had any dinner. Let me open a tin of soup while you talk to the detective.''

Emily shook her head. Why didn't the ambulance come? The only time she had to relax was in the afternoon and evening when it was all over for the day. And yesterday, even that had been spoiled. . . .

"I'd like some tea,'' she said, suddenly grateful that Annie Ramsay was there. The policeman, tall and healthy, frightened her. Perhaps she should never have admitted to having seen Dorothea Cassidy at all the day before. As it was, there were secrets between her and Dorothea which could never be told. She remembered the last conversation between them and closed her eyes with pain and guilt. She turned sharply to the policeman.

"Would you like a cup of tea, Sergeant?''

Hunter nodded uncomfortably. ''That would be very nice,'' he said.

The room was very hot. Usually he teased old ladies, flirted with them, made them believe that they were young and attractive again. He realised immediately that Emily Bowman would not be taken in. He resented Ramsay for having sent him there. He should be out looking for real villains. It was inconceivable that this old lady could be capable of murder.

To hide his discomfort he sat on a hard-backed chair close to the table and took out his notebook.

"I understand that you saw Mrs. Cassidy yesterday afternoon," he said. "What time was that?"

"At about half-past one," Emily said.

"Were you expecting her?"

"No." Emily paused. "No, but I wasn't surprised to see her. She had taken into calling in if she was in the neighborhood." And that was true enough, she thought.

"So it was just a routine visit?"

"No," Emily said. "Not exactly. When she arrived, I was still waiting for the ambulance, just as I am now. Dorothea offered to take me into the hospital for treatment. I have to go every day." Then she added, as if she did not want to make too much of it. "At least every weekday."

Annie Ramsay had been listening to the conversation through the open kitchen door.

"I didn't know that," she shouted above the hissing of the kettle. "I didn't know Dorothea took you in to the General."

"No," Emily said. "Well. You don't know everything."

"It was kind of her, mind, to drive you all that way."

The patronizing note in Annie's voice stung Emily to reply.

"Not particularly," she said. "There was someone she had to see at the hospital anyway. I wasn't putting her out."

"How did Mrs. Cassidy seem?" Hunter asked, interrupting the conversation between the women.

"Well enough," Emily said, then feeling that was not quite enough: "Perhaps a bit quiet. Perhaps she was concerned about the person she had to visit at the General. Families were always a worry, she said. Perhaps she was lucky never to have had children."

"What did she mean by that?"

"I don't know," Emily said firmly. "I didn't like to pry."

83

"Did she mention her meeting at the hospital when she had brought you home?"

"No," Emily said. "She didn't stay. She saw me to my flat then went away. She's a busy woman."

"What time was that?"

"Half-past three." She was surprised that she lied so fluently and turned back to the window to hide her astonishment.

Annie Ramsay came in from the kitchen, carrying a tray with cups and saucers and a tin of biscuits. She set the tray on the table and handed a cup to her friend. The tea was stronger than Emily liked, but she took it gratefully and sipped at it.

"I've got an idea," Annie said, excited, not content just to watch the interview but wanting to push the action along. "Why doesn't Mr. Hunter take you into the General, dear? Then you can get your treatment without having to wait for the ambulance and you can show him where Mrs. Cassidy went." She paused, then whispered, "Perhaps he'll be able to discover a clue."

Then hopefully, because unlike Hunter she found the bustle and drama in hospitals attractive and because she had always been curious about where Emily Bowman went every day: "I could come with you. Keep you company while you're waiting. It would make a nice change for you."

She turned to Hunter, her eyes gleaming. "There, Sergeant, don't you think that's a good idea? My nephew would be proud of me."

Hunter felt that he had been trapped but saw little way out of it. Ramsay would expect him to make enquiries at the hospital if Dorothea Cassidy had arranged to meet some mysterious stranger there. Yet it seemed from what Emily had told him that the arrangement had hardly been definite. Dorothea had taken the opportunity to go to the hospital because Mrs. Bowman needed a lift. Would she have gone otherwise? It was impossible to tell, but Hunter thought he could work on the theory that Dorothea had known that the person she wanted to see would be in the hospital anyway. Who could it be? A patient? A member of staff? Or another voluntary worker?

Without waiting for Hunter's reply to her suggestion, Annie Ramsay was already helping Emily into her cardigan. Emily stood up stiffly and steadied herself by holding on to the back of her chair.

"Would that be convenient, Sergeant?" she said. She felt stronger. She had been frightened into weakness by a stupid nightmare. There was nothing now to be afraid of. She even felt more optimistic about going for the treatment. The whole thing was over so much more quickly going by car than in the ambulance. She was almost looking forward to the smooth ride through the dry countryside. If she could go by car every day, perhaps she would feel differently about everything. She should have thought of that before. She felt a sudden stab of self-pity. No, she thought. Someone else should have realised. All those people at church who come here to offer help and support. Why didn't one of them see how much easier it would be for me to go by car and offer me a lift? They're all soft words and no action.

Annie took Emily down in the lift while Hunter ran down the stairs. He said it was so he could get the car, have it waiting right outside the door for them, but both women sensed his revulsion, knew that he could not bear to be in an enclosed space with age and frailty. When the lift doors opened, he was there to meet them. He even offered his arm to Emily to help her out, though he was grateful when she refused to take it.

At the front door of the building Emily Bowman paused and looked around her.

"Where's Clive?" she demanded. "He should be here,

picking up the rubbish in the garden. I haven't seen him since this morning.''

"I don't know," Annie said soothingly. ''He's probably just wandered off. You know what lads are like.''

But Clive's absence seemed to disturb Emily. ''He should be here,'' she repeated, and in the car she fidgeted and took no pleasure in the trip into town.

8

In the mornings the waiting room of the radiotherapy centre was packed with people squashed two to a chair, leaning against the walls, sometimes sitting on the floor. Now, at midday, it was quieter, only half-full, and the people seemed unbothered about the wait. The door was propped open to let in the sunshine and some younger patients sat on the narrow strip of grass outside the building, their skirts hitched around their thighs to expose their legs to the sun. The girls were planning a trip to Otterbridge fair. The last night was always the best, they said, laughing. The rides were more expensive but the atmosphere was great. Behind a tea counter two elderly WRVS helpers stood and chatted lazily. Emily took her appointment card from her handbag and placed it facedown on the receptionist's desk. A nurse would come eventually to take the cards, and patients would be called to the treatment room in order of arrival.

Annie looked around her with undisguised curiosity.

"Eh, pet," she said. "Isn't it nice in here? Easy chairs and carpet and everything." She lowered her voice to a whisper. "And don't the folks look *normal*."

"What did you expect?" Emily snapped, something of her old spirit returning. "It isn't a zoo."

87

"No, well . . ." Annie stared at a young man with a bald head and purple paint marks on his neck, who was doing the *Times* crossword with outstanding speed.

Hunter had gone to park the car and appeared awkwardly at the door. He regarded the girls, laughing in the sunshine, with something like fear. Were they mad? What did they have to laugh about? Annie and Emily settled into chairs and he stood and looked down at them.

"Tell me," he said, "did Mrs. Cassidy give you any idea where she was going?"

Emily shook her head. "No," she said. "She was rather mysterious. Usually she was very open, you know. She'd tell you anything. But not yesterday." She felt no obligation to this young man. Let him find out for himself, she thought.

"Was she away for a long time?"

"Not more than half an hour, possibly less. She was here when I came back from treatment."

"How did she seem?"

"Worried," Emily said. "Upset."

He was daunted by the task ahead of him. "It's a huge hospital," he said. "She could have gone anywhere."

"Oh no," Emily said. "I don't think so. You see, if she was going to one of the other departments, she would have gone outside. This building is quite self-contained. But she didn't. She went through that door over there."

She nodded towards the door which led into the rest of the building.

Hunter looked at the old lady curiously. She seemed to find the exchange amusing, as if she were playing some sort of game with him. It must be her age, he decided. Or her illness.

As they stared at the door a radiographer in a white tunic walked through and called out a list of names. Mrs. Bowman was the last on the list. She stood up slowly and followed two old men through the door. Hunter went after them.

The building was organised along a series of long corridors with intersections at right angles like an American street plan. The three patients had disappeared. Hunter walked along a spotless corridor past rows of shut doors. There was the faint hum of machinery and suddenly the incongruous sound of uninhibited laughter, which only added to his unease. He was looking for some senior administrator who might publicize Dorothea's presence in the hospital and ask for witnesses, but he felt unable to knock at one of the closed doors to ask for help. There were frightening symbols indicating radioactivity and implying that all visitors without detailed scientific knowledge should stay away. He wandered on, hoping to come to a reception area or to meet someone not wearing a white coat. He came at last, with some relief, to a plump woman in a uniform overall who moved a huge polisher from side to side across the linoleum tiles.

"Excuse me!" he shouted.

She pushed a button with her foot and the polisher whirred to a stop. He took a photograph of Dorothea Cassidy from his pocket.

"This woman was a visitor here yesterday afternoon," he said. "Did you see her?"

She leant on the polisher, grateful for an excuse to stop work. She looked carefully at the photograph.

"No," she said regretfully. "Sorry. But if she was a visitor, she would have gone upstairs. That's where the wards are."

"I see," he said. "I thought everyone came here as outpatients."

"No. Some of them are very poorly and have to stay in." She showed him the lift, then reluctantly started the machine and continued her work.

In Hastings Ward it was the calm, quiet time of early afternoon. All the activity of the morning was over and the patients had finished lunch. In the main room eight elderly

89

women dozed on their beds. It was hot and the flowers on the bedside cabinets drooped. Staff Nurse Imogen Buchan sat in the office and hoped that now she would have time to collect her thoughts and banish the panic which had overwhelmed her for two days. She knew she would have to come to a decision quickly. There was danger in this delay and confusion and there was not only herself to consider. But almost as soon as she had sat down behind the desk, the student nurse appeared, swinging insolently on the door, demanding her attention.

"Can you come and talk to Mrs. Peters," the student said. "She's the one that had the implant yesterday. She's suddenly decided that she's claustrophobic and can't possibly spend four days in that room." She touched the side of her head with her forefinger and raised her eyebrows. "Neurotic cow."

Imogen looked at the student with disapproval but said nothing. She walked along the corridor to the patient's cubicle. The student had disappeared probably to the cloakroom for a sneaky cigarette. Mrs. Peters's door was open, but the space was blocked by a heavy lead screen, shoulder high, a protection against radioactivity. At one time Imogen would have ignored the screen, gone past it to sit on the bed and take the woman's hand in an attempt to calm her. But today she stood in the corridor and looked across to the woman who lay moodily on top of the bed. The patient was in her early fifties, well groomed, articulate. She reminded Imogen strikingly of her mother. Her nightdress was open at the neck and Imogen could see the radioactive wire, held in place by brightly coloured beads, which was being used to treat the scar which remained after surgery.

"I'm sorry," the woman said, her voice high and hysterical. "I would never have agreed to this if I'd known what's involved. I'm so bored I could scream. It's like being a prisoner. I never could stand being shut in."

For a split second there was a glorious possibility that

Imogen would lose her temper. She wanted to scream back at the woman and tell her that she was self-centred, egotistical, self-dramatizing. But she maintained her precarious self-control. She had lost her temper with Dorothea Cassidy and that had been a disaster.

She spoke to the woman soothingly. She said Mrs. Peters had to stay where she was for the safety of the other patients and the staff. Soon it would all be over. The woman relaxed, reassured by the attention.

"I've been so silly," she said.

"Yes," Imogen said, under her breath, as she returned to the office.

Hunter stepped out of the lift into bright sunshine and felt immediately happier. He was faced by an empty dayroom and an open door into an office where a staff nurse was writing. All the ill people were decently out of sight. The nurse looked up and gave him an impatient professional smile. She was pretty in a pale, washed-out way. She should use more makeup, he thought. It would make all the difference. He smiled back at her and glanced automatically to the hand on the desk to see if she was wearing a wedding ring. He had always fancied women in uniform.

"Can I help you?" she asked.

Too right, he thought. There's a lot you could do for me.

"I'm sorry to disturb you," he said. "I'm Gordon Hunter from Northumbria police. We're trying to trace the movements of a woman. She was in this building yesterday and may have come to visit one of the patients on your ward."

As he approached her he could see that she looked very tired. The skin under her eyes was bruised and strained.

"Why do you want to know?" she asked.

"She was found murdered in Prior's Park early this morning," he said. "I expect you'll have heard about it."

She shook her head. "No," she said. "How terrible! I

was on an early shift this morning and I didn't know." There was no emotion in her voice and he thought that nurses, like policemen, were accustomed to sudden death.

He set the photograph on the desk. It was a recent picture of Dorothea and it had been taken by her husband. She was sitting at her desk, rather serious, as if she had been disturbed while working. Hunter watched the nurse glance down at it. She turned suddenly very pale and he realised that she was exhausted. It was a bloody shame, he thought, that nurses were so overworked. How could a man persuade one to go out with him if she was dead on her feet.

"No," she said at last, "I'm sorry. I don't recognise her. But she might have been on the ward yesterday afternoon. I don't see all the patients' visitors. We're very flexible about visiting here. Some of them have to travel long distances. They come and go pretty much as they please."

"Yes," he said. "I see." He was tempted to ask her if she was busy tonight, if she felt like a Chinese meal and a few drinks, but he could tell there would be little point.

"Were there any other nurses on the ward yesterday?" he asked.

"Of course," she said. "But none of them are here now. I swapped my shift."

"What about domestics?"

"I don't know," she said, apparently not very interested. "You could ask the supervisor."

"Doctors?"

"I think Rosie Steward, the registrar, was here," she said. "But she'd have nothing to do with the visitors."

It was a wild-goose chase, he thought. Just as he'd anticipated.

"I'll have to get the photograph circulated," he said. "If she was here, someone must have seen her. Who should I ask about that?"

She pointed him back down the stairs, pleased, he thought, to be left alone in the sunshine to her work.

When Hunter returned to the waiting room, Annie Ramsay and Emily Bowman were there, sitting together against one wall, drinking tea from polystyrene cups. The room was almost empty now and the WRVS ladies were clearing up and counting the money from the till. The nurse behind the desk was reading a romantic magazine. When he came in through the door, Annie Ramsay jumped up and waved to him, though it would have been impossible for him to miss them.

"That's good timing," she said brightly. "Mrs. Bowman's just come out of her treatment, haven't you, hinnie? We'll finish our tea and then we can be off." She looked at Hunter with her small and curious eyes. "Did you have any luck?"

He grunted noncommittally and shuffled his feet to show that he was a busy man and wanted to be away.

"No," Annie Ramsay said. "I didn't think you would." She turned to Emily Bowman and added with malice and enjoyment: "Such a pity our Stephen couldn't come. I say there's nothing to beat *experience*."

She helped Emily to her feet and imperiously sent Hunter to fetch the car.

Upstairs on the ward, staff nurse Imogen Buchan left the office, locked herself in the lavatory, and was sick. She ran the tap to hide the noise she was making, then washed her hands and began to splash water over her face. When she returned to the office, the student was there, leaning against the desk. When she saw Imogen, she began talking in a bored, complaining way about her boyfriend. He was so jealous, she said. She only had to look at another man and he was furious. You'd think he intended to kill her. Imogen sent her back onto the ward with menu cards and closed the door.

She knew the number of St. Mary's Vicarage, Otterbridge, without having to look it up and dialled with trembling fingers. Outside, people were starting to arrive for the afternoon's visiting and she realised she could be disturbed at any time, yet still she kept the receiver to her ear and prayed that someone would reply.

Please, she pleaded to herself. It can't be true. Let there be some mistake.

But when she left the hospital at the end of her shift, there were pictures of Dorothea Cassidy on every notice board. The woman's eyes seemed to be following her down the corridor, so Imogen felt that even after her death there was no escape from her.

9

W_{hen} Ramsay had first come to Otter-
bridge to work, he had been surprised that such a prosperous
town should tolerate an estate like the Ridgeway. Surely, he
thought, the rate payers would demand that it be tidied up,
that the graffiti should be removed. But although the Ridgeway Residents' Association did their best, they had little
power and the estate was invisible to the rest of the town.
There were no through roads and the only glimpse the more
affluent residents of Otterbridge had of it was from the train,
and then the houses were hidden by the old cars and decaying
furniture which had been tipped down the embankment.

Hilary Masters drove onto the estate without comment.
Outside the community centre a small crowd was gathered
to watch the decoration of a lorry for the carnival parade that
evening. The theme for the event was Otterbridge, Ancient
and Modern, and there were people trying on peculiar tunics
which Ramsay thought were supposed to be Roman togas.
The scene was chaotic, good-humoured. It was school
lunchtime and an elderly lollipop man leant on his stick and
watched them drive past. In the playground boys defied the
heat and chased after a football. On every corner there was
a scruffy ice-cream van, and through the open car windows
Ramsay could hear the conflicting tunes of their chimes. Out-

side the houses women sat on the pavements and chatted. They took no notice of Hilary's smart new car. They were used to social workers in the Ridgeway.

Theresa Stringer's garden came as something of a shock. The grass was brown and straggly through lack of water, like all the others in the street, but there was a pond, with a concrete bridge across it and a pair of gnomes with fishing rods.

"That's Joss Corkhill's influence," Hilary said. "He probably dreamt it up after a night at the pub and spent hours building it. He's like a kid."

The front door of the house was open and Ramsay could see a hall with bare floorboards leading to a small kitchen. There, Theresa Stringer and her son sat at a painted wooden table eating chips from newspaper. Ramsay recognised the teenager who had been lurking in the Armstrong House garden when he went to see his aunt.

Hilary stopped on the doorstep and called in: "Theresa, it's me, Miss Masters. Can we come in?"

Theresa Stringer left the table and walked down the hall to meet them. She was tiny, as slight and slim as a ten-year-old. She wore a T-shirt dress in red and black, Dennis the Menace stripes. Her hair was dark and short and she wore bright red plastic earrings. There was something of the hyperactive child about her. She was restless, perpetually on the move. But she was not stupid. That was clear to Ramsay from the start, and her bright intelligence surprised him. He had expected her to be more of a victim. She regarded Hilary aggressively.

"What are you doing here?" she demanded. "I thought Mr. Peacock was coming today." Then: "What have you done with my Beverley. I thought you were my friend. How could you let them take her away?"

"Beverley's fine," Hilary said gently. "I phoned the foster parents before I came out. They say she had a good night's

96

sleep and she's settling well. They're taking her to the beach later today."

"It's not fair," Theresa said. "I can't afford things like that for the bairn."

"She can come home on Monday," Hilary Masters said, "if you give up that crazy idea of going away with Joss."

"You don't understand," Theresa cried. "I love him."

There was an intimacy between the women which was more like friendship than the professional relationship between social worker and client. They had nothing superficial in common, but they spoke to each other honestly, as equals. Again Ramsay was surprised. He felt he had misjudged Hilary completely.

"Do you?" Hilary said. "It would never work."

"How do you know?" Theresa demanded. "You don't even know him. You won't give it a chance."

"I'm sorry," Hilary said. "We have to talk to you. Can't we come in?"

Theresa shrugged and moved away from the door to let them into a living room. There was a square of carpet in the middle of the floor, a sofa and a television, but no other furniture. Despite that, the room had a cluttered and claustrophobic feel. There were magazines on the floor, toys in a blue plastic washing basket in one corner. On one wall was a replica poster for Barnum's Circus, on another an Irish Tourist Board print of mountains and sea. In a small, round glass bowl on the mantel shelf three goldfish swam listlessly.

"Joss brought those back for Beverley from the fair," Theresa said. "She loved them." She pointed suspiciously at Ramsay. "Who's he?"

"This is Inspector Ramsay," Hilary said. "He wants to ask you some questions."

"Why?" Theresa demanded, suddenly frightened. "I told you. Joss didn't touch her, I was here all the time."

"This isn't about Joss," Hilary said quickly. "Not now. The inspector's here to talk to you about Mrs. Cassidy."

"What's Dorothea been up to?" Theresa said. "Been arrested, has she, for not paying her poll tax? She said it was unfair and she wasn't going to pay."

"Didn't Clive tell you?" Hilary said, shocked. "Mrs. Cassidy's dead."

"No," Theresa said, shaking her head slowly. "He didn't say a thing."

"Mrs. Cassidy was found murdered early this morning in Prior's Park," Ramsay said formally. "We're making enquiries about her movements yesterday. I understand that she was here?"

But Theresa was unable to reply. She flung herself onto the sofa and began to cry. Ramsay watched the thin blades of her shoulders move under the cotton dress. Hilary sat beside her and began to stroke her hair away from her face until she sat up abruptly.

"Who killed her?" she asked. "Who was it?"

"We don't know," Ramsay said. "Not yet. That's why I'm here. Are you well enough to answer some questions?"

Theresa nodded.

"Was she here yesterday afternoon?"

"It was about dinner time," she said.

"Why did Mrs. Cassidy come to see you?"

"She promised she would," Theresa said quickly. "She said as soon as the case conference was over she'd come and tell me what had happened." She looked angrily at Hilary. "Mrs. Cassidy was on my side," she said. "She didn't want Beverley taken away."

"Theresa!" Hilary said quietly. "I'm on your side. You know that."

Ramsay ignored the interruption and continued:

"Why did Mrs. Cassidy come and not your social worker?"

"Mr. Peacock, the social worker, came with her," Theresa said. "In his own car but at the same time. He came to collect Beverley." She paused and Ramsay expected another outburst of tears, but surprisingly she smiled. "He didn't like coming here on his own," she said mischievously. "He was frightened of Joss when he'd been drinking. Mrs. Cassidy wasn't frightened of anything."

"So Mr. Peacock came to take Beverley to the foster parents and Mrs. Cassidy stayed here to talk to you?"

Theresa nodded.

"What did you talk about?"

Theresa looked to Hilary Masters for reassurance and then answered with jerky bursts of speech.

"She wanted to know about everything," she said. "Mrs. Cassidy was that kind of woman. All questions. When she first came here to see Clive, I thought she was one of those nosy do-gooders. What does she want to come up here for? I thought. Why mix with the likes of us? She's not even paid for it. But she was canny. She wasn't how I expected." She paused, but Ramsay said nothing. He hoped to re-create his image of Dorothea from these incoherent ramblings.

There were footsteps on the pavement outside and Theresa jumped up and looked out.

"Are you expecting Joss?" Hilary asked. "Where is he?"

"On the abbey meadow," Theresa said defiantly. "Working on the fair. He'll come home this afternoon, then go back to work with his mate this evening. It's the last night. They'll be busy."

"Will he come home?" Hilary asked quietly. "Or will he go to the pub? Drink all his wages."

"He'll come home!" Theresa said. "He promised."

But the footsteps outside the house seemed to have unsettled her, and though she returned to the sofa, her attention was elsewhere. There was a silence, then the sound of a baby crying through the thin walls from next door.

"You were talking to me about Mrs. Cassidy," Ramsay prompted. "She asked lots of questions. Was she an easy person to talk to?"

With some effort Theresa directed her attention away from the window and back to him.

"Yes," she said. "I didn't like her coming at first. I knew she was a vicar's wife. I told her at the beginning: 'You might persuade our Clive to come to your church but you'll not get me inside.' "

"What did she say to that?" Ramsay asked.

"She laughed," Theresa said. "There was nothing you could say to offend her. She said there were more important things than going to church."

"Tell me about yesterday," Ramsay persisted. "What exactly did you talk about then? When Mr. Peacock left you alone."

Then suddenly Theresa went mysterious. It was none of Ramsay's business what they talked about, she said. It had nothing to do with him.

"But you must have talked about Joss," Ramsay said. "She must have wanted to know what happened between Joss and Beverley."

"She believed me!" Theresa said defensively. "She believed it was an accident."

"Theresa," Hilary Masters said. "Did you tell Mrs. Cassidy how Beverley got those bruises?"

"Yes!" Theresa shouted defiantly. "I told her everything. You couldn't lie to her."

"Why didn't you tell Mr. Peacock before the case conference? Or me?"

Theresa shrugged.

"Mr. Peacock doesn't like Joss," she said. "He'd always believe the worse of him."

Ramsay interrupted quietly.

"What *did* happen, Miss Stringer?" he said. "You do realise that you'll have to tell us."

Theresa crouched on the sofa, her knees by her chin, her red-and-black dress stretched over them.

"Joss was pissed," she said. "It was before the fair came and he was fed up, bored. He couldn't get work. We had a row."

"What about?" Hilary asked.

"I can't remember exactly how it started," Theresa said. "It doesn't matter now."

Ramsay thought she would be a fighter and imagined the pair of them, the alcoholic man and the tiny woman, hurling insults from one room to another, throwing things, waking the baby, confusing Clive. Probably they both enjoyed the drama of it, he thought. A good row would clear the air, get rid of some of Corkhill's frustration. Only the children would be terrified.

"When was this?" he asked.

"About a fortnight ago. It was in the evening. Joss had had a win on the horses and had been drinking all day. I'd been here with Beverley. It didn't seem right that he'd been out enjoying himself. I wouldn't have minded a change."

"Where were the children when this was happening?"

"Clive was in his bedroom, reading comics. I was getting Bev ready for bed. When I heard Joss come in, I sent her upstairs."

"Did you often row when Joss had been drinking?"

"No," she said, desperate for him to understand. "He's not violent, not really. Usually we have a laugh. Or he goes to sleep."

"But that night he picked a fight."

"I don't know," she said, then added honestly: "I expect I picked the fight. Because I'd been in all day with the bairn."

"If you and Mr. Corkhill were arguing here and the children were upstairs, how did Beverley come to be hurt?"

101

"She must have been frightened by the noise. By that time Joss was throwing things around. We were in the kitchen. We didn't hear her come downstairs. She just appeared at the door. Then she ran between us and held on to me, crying. Joss wanted to move her out of the way, to get at me. He didn't mean to hurt her."

"What did he do?"

"He picked her up and threw her to one side. She hit her head and her cheek on the oven and her ribs on the floor."

Throughout the exchange Hilary had been watching Theresa anxiously, like some defense solicitor, Ramsay thought, who is frightened a client will incriminate herself. Did she know more about Theresa's relationship with Dorothea than she was letting on? With the last admission she seemed almost relieved. Perhaps she felt that now her decision to take Beverley into care had been justified.

"You do see," Hilary said, "that it makes no difference whether Joss meant to hurt her or not. He might have killed her."

"I know," Theresa said. "That's what Dorothea told me."

"Did she give you any idea what you should do next?" Ramsay asked quietly.

"She said I couldn't go with Joss to work on the fair." Theresa spoke reluctantly. She was still attracted, Ramsay could tell, by the romance of the idea. "She said that was impossible if I wanted to have Beverley back."

"We'd all told you that," Hilary said with some irritation. "You didn't believe us!"

"She said I had to tell Joss that I wouldn't go with him as soon as I saw him. If I left it, I would find it harder. If he loved me enough, he would stay. If he didn't, I was strong enough to carry on by myself. She would be there to help me."

She turned to them, her eyes filling with tears again. "But she won't," she said. "Not now."

102

"Did you do as Mrs. Cassidy suggested and talk to Mr. Corkhill as soon as he got home yesterday afternoon?" Ramsay said.

"Oh yes!" she said. "I thought I was so brave. I told him, all right."

"What happened?"

"There was a scene," she said. "He was furious. No interfering old bat was going to tell him what to do. He was going to leave with the fair when it goes at the weekend. It was up to me to decide whether or not I wanted to go with him. He'd give me until tonight to decide."

"So he was very angry?" Ramsay said. "Was he violent?"

"Not with me," she said. "He blamed Mrs. Cassidy." Ramsay thought she was going to say more, but she must have realised the implication of the question and her voice trailed off.

Outside, a small girl with tangled hair pedalled furiously down the pavement on a tricycle. They watched her hoist on a handlebar to turn a corner.

"I'm surprised that Mrs. Cassidy didn't stay and talk to Mr. Corkhill with you," Ramsay said slowly. "It seems unlike her that she would expect you to face him alone."

"She wanted to visit an old lady," Theresa said defensively. "Someone with cancer. She offered to stay, but I told her to go. I was afraid of what Joss might do. . . ."

Again she stopped, frightened.

"What were you afraid of?" Ramsay asked. "What did you think he might do?"

"I don't know," she said. "Not what you think. Joss couldn't have killed her. He wouldn't do a thing like that. . . ." But there was uncertainty in her voice. Ramsay would have liked to reassure her, but he was beginning to feel the excitement of a conclusion to the case.

"So Mrs. Cassidy went and left you here to wait for Joss," he said. "What time was that?"

She shook her head. There was no clock in the house. She had nothing to be on time for.

"I don't know," she said. "One o'clock. Half-past."

Ramsay hesitated. It still seemed uncharacteristic that Dorothea Cassidy would leave a woman who had just lost her daughter to face a potentially violent man alone. With a sudden inspiration he said:

"She arranged to come back later, didn't she? After she had visited the old lady in Armstrong House?"

Theresa nodded reluctantly. This is it, Ramsay thought. This is the end of it. Dorothea came back to the Ridgeway and Joss was waiting for her, still drunk, his pride hurt, wanting an argument. Dorothea had stood up to him because she was, as Theresa said, frightened of nothing. And he had strangled her, frustrated and furious because she had wrecked his dream of taking Theresa travelling.

"What time did Mrs. Cassidy come back?" he said gently. He felt sorry for Theresa. He thought she was about to lose everything.

Theresa looked toward Hilary Masters as if only a woman could help her, but Hilary stood up suddenly and moved to the window, looking out.

"Teatime," she said. "About half-past four. The children's programmes had started on the telly."

"Was there another row?" Ramsay asked. "Between her and Mr. Corkhill?"

"No," Theresa said. "How could there be? Joss wasn't here. He stormed out earlier. I thought I would never see him again."

"But you did see him again? He did come home last night?"

She nodded.

"What time did he come home?"

104

"I don't know. Very late. I'd fallen asleep in front of the television."

"How did he seem? Was he still angry?"

"No," she said. "Pissed, sentimental. You know how they get."

"Did he tell you where he'd been last night?"

"To work," she said. "To the fair. Then to the pub with his mates."

"Did he mention Mrs. Cassidy?" Ramsay asked.

"No," she said. "It was if he'd forgotten about her. Or as if it didn't matter anymore."

Ramsay looked at Hilary Masters. She had regained her pose of cool detachment. She turned back into the room, unmoved, it seemed, by Theresa's distress. He supposed it was the only way she could survive the demands of her job. Dorothea had remained human, accessible, involved, and she was dead.

"If you don't mind, we'll wait until Mr. Corkhill comes home," Ramsay said. "Then we'll take him down to the station to ask him some questions. And I'd like some scientists to look at your house. It won't cause you any inconvenience."

Theresa stared blankly ahead of her and he could not tell if she had understood him. The three of them sat in silence, watching the dust in the sunlight, waiting for the footsteps on the pavement which would mean that Joss Corkhill was on his way home.

10

In the bus from Armstrong Street to the Ridgeway, Clive Stringer stared at Walter Tanner and grinned. They got off the bus at the same stop and Clive hurried home. He saw the old man again, a little later, when he went to fetch chips for himself and his mother. Tanner was standing outside the row of shops at the centre of the estate. He waited until Clive had bought the chips and disappeared back up the road until he made his move.

Walter Tanner had started coming to the betting shop on the Ridgeway Estate when his mother was still alive. He had chosen the Ridgeway because it was unlikely that he would meet any of his acquaintances there, and in those days, before he had gambled away all the family money, he had owned a car. His mother was one of those women who became elderly in middle age and who suffer from persistent and undefined illnesses. When Walter's father was alive, there was some controlling her. She accepted his authority with resentment but not hostility and saw it as her duty to prepare him meals and help him occasionally in the shop. But Walter's father had died in late middle age and then she became almost permanently an invalid. She left her room in the evenings to watch television, which she enjoyed, but took no active part in the household. Walter found himself hating her and hating himself because he could find no compassion for her. He took his religion seriously.

At first the trips to the betting shop were weekly. Inside, in the hot and smoky little room, he felt anonymous. He could take any risk he liked and no one would know. Then he became recognised as a regular, one of the gang, and he found a warmth and friendship he had never experienced in church. As a single man in church, he was isolated, exceptional. The place seemed full of happy families or gaggles of elderly ladies. He felt more an employee of the congregation than a participating member. There was no social contact. The bookmaker's was full of single men, and they accepted Walter without question. He was terribly unlucky and they loved him for it. No matter how much they lost, they could console themselves that Walter had lost more. When occasionally he did win, they were honestly pleased for him. They clapped him on the shoulder, told him his luck must be about to change. He felt that the weekly trips to the Ridgeway kept him sane. Without them, he would have murdered his mother. Soon once a week was not enough and his savings began to disappear.

His mother died without his assistance on the weekend after he had to sell the car. He felt surprisingly little emotion, not even relief, when he came home from the Ridgeway to find her cold and stiff in her bed. She still had the complaining, slightly petulant look on her face which was as much a part of her as the mole on her cheek and her watery brown eyes. He began automatically to wonder what he would back in the three-fifteen at Newmarket.

After his mother's death he tried to keep away from the betting shop for a while. He told himself that now he had no reason to escape. But he was wrong. There were other pressures. He cared about the shop and wanted to maintain it in its old glory, but it was expensive to run and his customers grew older and less willing to spend money.

Soon he was in debt. More disturbingly Dorothea Cassidy turned up at the vicarage and began to question his authority in the only place he had ever had any power. Eventually he sold the business, and then, even with the gambling, he had a little financial security. Dorothea Cassidy was less easy to deal with.

When Dorothea's car was found on his drive, the instinct to escape to the betting shop was irresistible. He felt that in the accepting, unquestioning atmosphere of the shop he would find the strength to sort himself out and decide what to do. After a few bets he would relax again. But when he pushed open the door and waved his usual greeting to Susan behind the counter, he found they were all talking about the murder.

"Here's Wally," one of the punters said. "He'll know what's going on. Tell us about it, Wally."

In comparison with them he was well educated and had a limitless supply of money. They trusted his judgement. They gathered around him, wanting information, and it was almost the same sensation as after a win.

"Well," he said, diffident, in case they should think he was boasting. "Actually her car was found on my drive."

Then he was the most popular person in the place. Was there blood? they wanted to know. Had the police given him a bad time? Perhaps he could sell the story to the papers and make a fortune.

On the abbey meadow the fair was still. Men cleared up the mess of the night before. They called to each other, using nicknames and the technical terms of their trade which would have been incomprehensible to outsiders. Joss Corkhill walked among them, an Alsatian as big as a wolf by his side, shouting greetings, feeling immensely at home. He told himself the fair was the only place he had ever belonged. It was his Irish blood, he thought. He needed to travel. He regarded each of the rides with affection. He passed the waltzers where the night before teenage couples had clung to each other, shrieking with mock terror above the music, and the galloping horses and the old-fashioned helter-skelter with its wooden slide and woven rope mats. His mate's ride was called the Noah's Ark. Carved animals spun at great speed around an undulating track. There was nothing heavy to do. Most of the work was in setting up the fair and packing it away at the end, but Joss was occupied all morning in cleaning and general maintenance, and when they packed up at dinner time, his friend gave him ten pounds.

As he worked, Joss tried to decide what to do about Theresa. He wanted her with him. It was a matter of pride. He had thought he had persuaded her and then the bloody social worker and the bloody vicar's wife had got in the way. Yet as he walked round the wooden animals, he smiled to himself.

"You're in a good mood today," his mate said. Usually, before he had had a few drinks, Joss was bad-tempered, taciturn, inclined to lash out.

Once, after a court appearance for being drunk and disorderly, a well-meaning magistrate had asked for a social enquiry report to get to the root of his drinking and his violent mood swings. The probation officer had sent him to a psychiatrist, but the doctor had failed to come up with a convenient label. Corkhill had a personality disorder, he said, and they could do nothing to treat that. So he had been fined and sent away to continue drinking.

Rumours of the murder across the river came early but were not specific. By the time the police came to the abbey meadow with their photographs and their suspicion of everyone who worked on the fair, Joss Corkhill had left the site and was spending his wages in one of the pubs in the town, his Alsatian under the bench at his feet. He drank quickly and heavily, but he did not stay long. He wanted to talk to Theresa. It was time, he thought, for a showdown.

The streets in the centre of town were busy with Friday shoppers and visitors. Joss Corkhill pushed his way through them and walked quickly out of the town towards the Ridgeway Estate, stopping on the way at a small off-licence to buy a bottle of cider. At the corner of the street where Theresa lived, he paused. There was a smart car he did not recognise outside. It was probably the social worker's boss, he thought. That was all he needed. Another bloody woman. So he took a drink from the bottle and went back to the bookmaker's, thinking that he would wait until the visitor had gone.

At the door of the betting shop he stopped and let the dog in first. He liked to make an entrance. But when he followed, no one had noticed that the dog was there. The regulars were gathered together in a huddle like a bunch of old women and they talked excitedly not of horses but of Dorothea Cassidy's murder.

"She was here yesterday afternoon, you know," one said. "Down at the Stringers. There's a policeman in the house now. He came with the social worker. I saw them."

"There are cops all over the place asking questions."

Without speaking, Corkhill called to the dog and left. He walked to the Otterbridge bypass and stood by the side of the road to hitch a lift.

In the kitchen of his mother's house Clive Stringer hungrily ate his chips. He gathered together the greasy paper in an untidy ball and thrust it into the cardboard box in the corner which served as a bin. I should have stayed at Armstrong House, he thought. I would have been safer there. How did they get onto me so quickly? The kitchen door was still wide open and the living-room door was ajar, so he could hear the murmur of voices as the policeman talked to his mother and Miss Masters, but in his panic he could not make out the

110

words. I should get away, he thought. But escape seemed impossible. There was no backdoor from the kitchen and the windows would not open since the council workmen had painted the frames two years ago. His only way out was through the front. Why don't they come and get me? he thought. What are they doing? At last his confinement in the kitchen was unbearable. The voices in the living room had stopped and that added to his tension. He walked carefully sideways out into the hall, sliding his back against the wall in a futile attempt to make himself invisible. He had reached the front door and was lifting his hand to the catch when the inspector spoke.

"Clive!" he said, and the sudden sound of the stern voice in the quiet house made Clive's heart pound and his legs shake. "I hope you weren't intending to leave without talking to us. Why don't you come in with us?"

The boy stood, still with his back to the wall, staring through the crack in the door towards them.

"Come in, Clive," Hilary Masters said. "There's nothing to be afraid of."

The boy sidled into the room and looked at them with frightened, unfocused eyes.

"Sit down, Clive," Hilary Masters said. "The police inspector wants to ask you some questions." He sat on the edge of the settee. He was shaking.

"You mustn't be frightened," Hilary said. "The police don't think you've done anything wrong. They just want your help."

Clive heard the words as if they came from a great distance away, but knew that it was all a trick. He would have to be clever or they would catch him out.

"I haven't done anything," he said.

"Of course not, Clive," Hilary said reassuringly. "Just listen to the inspector and answer his questions."

111

"Clive," Ramsay said. "I understand that Mrs. Cassidy was a friend of yours."

The boy nodded cautiously. "She took me to the youth club," he said. "And then I went to church with her."

"When did you last see her?" Ramsay asked.

Clive thought carefully. He had to be dead clever, he thought again.

"Yesterday afternoon," he said. "At Armstrong House."

"You were working at Armstrong House yesterday afternoon?"

"Yes," he said. He sat, his mouth open, staring.

"What were you doing?" Ramsay asked, trying to control his impatience.

"Cleaning the corridors and the stairs."

"So you would have seen anyone coming and going?"

He nodded.

"What was Mrs. Cassidy doing at Armstrong House?"

Clive thought carefully again, weighing up the answer before he decided there was no harm in the truth.

"She'd come to visit Mrs. Bowman," he said. "She came to visit her a lot. Sometimes once, twice a week."

"Can you tell the time?" Ramsay asked.

"Of course!" Clive was indignant. "And I've got a watch. Mrs. Cassidy gave it me last birthday."

"Were you wearing your watch yesterday?"

"I always wear it," he said simply.

"So you'll be able to tell me what time Mrs. Cassidy arrived at Armstrong House yesterday afternoon and what time she left," Ramsay said.

"She came at half-past one," Clive said proudly, his guard dropping more with each question. "I'd finished my dinner. If I'm there all day, the warden gives me dinner. It was shepherd's pie."

"And when did she go?" Ramsay asked.

"Straightaway," Clive said. "The ambulance hadn't come

to take Mrs. Bowman to the hospital, so Mrs. Cassidy said she'd give her a lift.''

"Did Mrs. Cassidy bring Mrs. Bowman back to Armstrong House?"

The boy nodded.

"I don't suppose you have any idea what time that was."

"Half-past three!" Clive said, triumphant. "It was half-past three."

"How are you so certain?" Ramsay asked.

"I'd been waiting for her," Clive said. "I liked to see her. She always cheered me up like when I saw her."

"What did you do then?" Ramsay asked. "Did she take Mrs. Bowman to her room?"

"Yes," he said. "I helped her."

"And then," Ramsay said, "I suppose Mrs. Cassidy left Armstrong House."

"No," Clive said. "I saw her go into Mrs. Bowman's room, but I never saw her leave. I waited for Mrs. Cassidy. Sometimes she gave me a lift home—the warden doesn't mind me going early if all the work's done. I waited until four o'clock and then I walked into town and got the bus."

"Perhaps you missed her," Ramsay suggested. "Perhaps you were working and didn't see her go."

But Clive was quite positive.

"No!" he said. "I'd finished my work by then and I was waiting for her, sitting on the bottom of the stairs. I was bound to have seen her even if she'd come in the lift. Bound to."

Theresa Stringer had been following the conversation. "He's telling the truth," she said. "I told you Dorothea didn't get here until half-past four. She left just before Clive came home."

"Could she have met Mr. Corkhill in the street?"

113

"No," she cried. "I've told you Joss wouldn't have wanted to hurt her."

Ramsay ignored the outburst and turned back to Clive.

"Did you see Mrs. Cassidy again yesterday?" Ramsay asked.

"No," Clive said, thinking how clever he was, cleverer than any old policeman.

"What time did you get home?"

"About quarter past five."

"Did it take you a whole hour to walk from Armstrong House?"

Clive was beginning to enjoy himself. He looked at the inspector as if shocked by the man's lack of faith in him.

"I've told you," he said. "I walked into town. I hung around the shops there for a bit, then I got the bus home."

"Who was in the house when you got here?"

"No one," he said. "Only my mam."

"Did you go out again yesterday evening?"

There was a pause, and for a moment Clive was struck by a terrible panic.

"Well," Ramsay said. "Did you go out again yesterday evening?"

"Yes," Clive said at last. "I went to the fair."

"Did you see anyone you knew?"

Again there was a moment's hesitation. Then Clive answered. "Only Joss," he said. "He was in a good mood. He gave me some money."

"What time did you see Joss?" Ramsay asked.

"When I first got there. At about eight."

"What time did you get home?"

"Late," Clive said. "Really late." And despite the watch which Dorothea had given, it seemed that he could not be more specific than that.

They lapsed again into silence. Ramsay felt a mounting impatience. Where was Corkhill? Despite Theresa's insistence that Joss had not met Dorothea the afternoon before, he was still the most obvious suspect.

Clive stood up suddenly.

"I'm going back to work," he said. "To Armstrong House."

They heard the front door bang and saw him lope past the window on the way to town.

"I should go, too," Hilary Masters said. That decided Ramsay. He could not sit there, waiting, all afternoon. He put out a general alert for Corkhill on his personal radio and asked her to give him a lift back to the police station.

That afternoon Northumberland bus drivers went on strike after a dispute about overtime. Walter Tanner waited at the bus stop at the entrance of the Ridgeway for an hour before he realised that no bus was going to come. He was unused to vigorous exercise and the prospect of walking home dismayed him. The elation of his time at the bookmaker's had long since left him. It was three o'clock. The boys from the high school, let out early because it was carnival Friday, were wandering back to the estate in an aimless, can-kicking, gum-chewing group. Tanner waited until they passed before starting off down the hill to the town. Their undirected aggression frightened him.

It was very hot still and he felt his face burn with the exertion of walking. The road into town was busy with traffic, but there were no pedestrians and he was grateful at least for that. At last he came to the streets which were more familiar to him. Close to home, on a corner, a large public house was open. People holding long glasses were sitting in the garden under striped umbrellas. Tanner was tempted for a moment to go inside, to find a dark corner to sit and recover his composure with a pint of beer, but he knew he was in no state to meet anyone. It would be better, after all, to go straight home.

115

At the door he stood for a moment, his muscles trembling, almost faint. He felt in his trousers pocket for his keys and pushed one into the keyhole. He tried to turn it with shaking fingers before realising that the door was already unlocked. In the shock of finding Dorothea's car he must have gone out with the door still open. It hardly mattered. There was nothing inside worth stealing. He shut the door behind him and stood, breathing deeply, enjoying the cool of the house and the relief of being home.

Never again, he thought automatically. No more gambling. That must be the last time.

But as he began to relax he was already trying to find ways around the self-imposed ban. I could arrange everything on the telephone, he thought, though he knew he would miss the excitement and companionship which was as much part of the addiction as the thought of winning. I could just go on the big days.

He sat heavily on the bottom of the stairs and took off his shoes. One of his socks had a hole in the heel and his skin was red and blistered after the walk. He padded into the kitchen, filled a kettle, and set it on the gas stove. While he was waiting for it to boil he went upstairs to swill his hands and face.

He knew when he reached the top of the stairs that someone had been into the house because the bathroom door was open. With an instinctive embarrassment he always shut the bathroom door.

"Hello!" he shouted. "Is anyone there?"

He thought the police might be back. He had a vague idea that scientists came and did tests. There was no reply and he walked on into the bathroom.

Clive Stringer lay in the grimy bath in a pool of blood. He was curled like a child with his knees almost up to his chin. He had been stabbed in the back and his wrists had been cut.

It was too much for Walter Tanner. It was like a nightmare. The boy had been haunting him all day. He stood quite still. Downstairs the kettle howled.

11

A*t* the Walkers' house in the country the Cassidys were treated as invalids. Mrs. Walker even wanted to make them soup for lunch. Soup was comforting, she said. But her husband, a retired major with a limp and a surprisingly boyish face, would not hear of it.

"In this heat!" he said. "Don't be ridiculous!"

So she made one of her special salads and picked strawberries, then took the meal into the garden for them, on a tray. There the Cassidys sat on white wooden chairs in the dappled shadow of a willow tree, stunned and bewildered, unable to move. In the background was the house, square and white, with a dovecote and stables, and beyond that a wood where pheasants were reared. Major Walker was something big in the County Landowners Association, and in feudal Northumberland he was treated as a squire.

When the meal was over, the Walkers tactfully left the Cassidys alone and returned to the house. They watched the father and son through open French windows.

"Poor things," Dolly Walker said. "Poor dear things." She was a magistrate and her husband often told her she was too soft to sit on the bench. Sometimes, after a day in court, she would come home and cry at the stories she had heard.

"Yes," he said. "It's been a terrible shock." But he was

disturbed to find that he was not as shocked as he should have been and that there was, too, an uneasy sensation of relief. Now things could get back to normal again. Dorothea had been tremendous, of course. She had brought a breath of life to the whole church. What did his wife call it? A spirit of renewal? But there had been something unsettling about Dorothea. All that waving of her hands in the air during the singing of the hymns had unnerved him. He would never say anything to Dolly, who had become quite a new woman since Dorothea Cassidy had arrived, but he felt somehow that there was something pagan in such exhibitionism. Perhaps she had spent too long in Africa.

Then there was the tension between Dorothea and Walter Tanner. The major had never got to the bottom of Walter's problems. Walter was not the sort to confide and it had seemed wrong to him to pry. He was not a sensitive man and had never been aware of Walter's simmering resentment about the sharing of churchwardens' responsibilities, but the grocer's hounded, haunted look in Dorothea's presence touched Major Walker deeply. He would have liked to offer Walter help, but after a relationship of distant politeness he was not sure how to go about it.

"I'd almost say Patrick was taking it worse than his father," Dolly Walker said tentatively. She was usually good about people but too diffident to trust her own judgement. She was afraid of her husband's sarcasm. "He's not mentioned Dorothea since he arrived. I hope he doesn't feel responsible. People do, you know, quite irrationally, at times like these."

She was taking psychology A level at evening classes and felt almost an expert.

"Don't be ridiculous!" Major Walker said again. But as he looked out at the boy he could see what she meant. Edward Cassidy was limp and exhausted and wept openly, but

119

Patrick sat, gripping the arms of his chair and staring ahead of him with a rigid intensity.

There was something about the boy which irritated Major Walker. He thought the display of emotion must be a show. Dorothea was only the stepmother. They had not known each other very long. If she were his natural mother, the grief would be understandable. The Walkers had never had children and the major had a sentimental view of the parental relationship. He thought Patrick should have more self-control. Two years of National Service would make a man of him, he thought, but he said nothing. Dolly would accuse him of being heartless.

The Walkers had gone back to the house, ostensibly to fetch more wine, and now they filed back over the grass towards the Cassidys, the major in front carrying the wine in a bucket of ice. Like Beech, he thought. At Blandings. He was a great Woodhouse fan, and the memory of the books came as a welcome relief.

The remains of their meal were still on the table. Edward Cassidy had hardly eaten anything, though he had drunk several glasses of wine very quickly, and now when he spoke, his words were a little slurred and incoherent. Patrick had seemed ravenous, pushing forkfuls of food into his mouth in silence, then wiping his plate with a piece of bread. Dolly fussed and gathered the dirty plates onto a tray. The major stood to open the wine and was about to draw the cork from the bottle when Patrick Cassidy got suddenly to his feet, rocking the unsteady garden furniture, making the glasses rattle dangerously.

"I'm sorry," he said. "I can't stand this. I'll have to go." He blinked and his eyelashes showed very fair against his pink skin. He turned stiffly and walked across the lawn.

The vicar looked up from his empty glass. "Patrick," he said in confusion and surprise. "What is this about?"

120

But by then the boy had gone and gave no sign that he had heard.

Poor dear, Dolly thought. He's going to cry and he's too proud to let us see. The major, who had seen many young soldiers before him on disciplinary charges, thought he detected something else. Shame perhaps. Or guilt.

They watched until Patrick disappeared to the back of the house where the cars were parked, then they heard the sound of the engine as he drove too quickly toward the road and the squeal of brakes as he stopped at the end of the drive to let a tractor pass in the lane.

Dear God, the major thought. If he's not careful, he'll kill himself. Reckless young fool. Automatically he completed the process of opening the bottle and poured wine into Edward Cassidy's glass.

Edward Cassidy seemed not to notice and stared after his son with horror. He was suddenly taken up with the arrangements for his own return to Otterbridge.

"Oh dear," he said wretchedly. "Patrick's taken the car. Now how will I get home?"

He fidgeted and worried like a confused old person at a day centre who believes he has been deserted.

"Of course we'll take you back," Dolly said. "Or if you prefer, you can spend the night here." She found his selfish preoccupation with what was to become of him a little embarrassing. It was unlike him. Usually he had impeccable manners.

No, no, he said. There were so many things to do. He knew he was being a nuisance, but he would really rather be at home. Patrick, after all, would go back to the vicarage. They should be together. Perhaps if it wasn't too much trouble, they could go now. He stood up, his glass still in his hand, and waited for them to arrange it.

"Of course," Dolly said, and by now there were tears in her eyes. He was usually so confident, so able to put on a

121

good show. "We'll come with you and wait at the vicarage until Patrick comes home."

Then he turned on them and shouted, his voice querulous and pitiful.

"No," he cried. "You don't understand. I have to be on my own."

When he saw how offended and hurt they were, there was a brief show of the old charm. "I'm so sorry," he said. "You must forgive me. I'm really not myself today."

He drank the remainder of the wine in the glass and allowed Dolly to take his arm and lead him back toward the house.

They had a big BMW and sat him in the back of it, treating him still like an invalid. If it had not been so hot, Dolly would have tucked a rug around his knees. The major drove slowly, avoiding the potholes in the lane, and in Otterbridge they were held up by two men on stilts who paraded down the centre of front street. All the same, when they arrived at the vicarage, the church clock only showed two o'clock. Later, when the police asked questions about the time, Dolly was tempted to lie, but the major told her that liars were always caught out and anyway it was impossible to believe that Patrick or Edward could have murdered that half-wit from Armstrong House. What motive could there be? The police asked, too, if Patrick was already back at the vicarage by the time they returned with the priest. Again, reluctantly, they told the truth. No, they said, there was no sign of Patrick's car when they saw Edward into the vicarage and sat him in the study, surrounded by his photographs of Dorothea.

Imogen Buchan finished her shift at the hospital at two o'clock. She changed quickly out of her uniform in the cloakroom then hurried away, past the smudged posters of Dorothea Cassidy, to the staff car park to collect her Metro. There were other nurses on her ward who had finished shift at the

122

same time and they lingered in the cloakroom, sharing gossip, planning some social event to which Imogen had not been invited. They took little notice when Imogen hurried away. One of them put a finger under her nose to express snootiness; they all giggled and returned to their conversation. They acknowledged that Imogen was a brilliant nurse, but she had never fitted in. If they had been closer friends, they would have known that Patrick Cassidy was her boyfriend. Someone might have recognised the connection with the murdered woman on the poster and told the police. But Imogen had always kept her private life to herself.

When she had decided on nursing as a career, her parents were, at the same time, disappointed and relieved. They would definitely have preferred her to go to university, but though they would never admit it to Imogen, they realised she was unlikely to get high enough A-level grades for a good university place. Her parents were both English teachers at the high school and had inside knowledge. Imogen's teachers said that she worked very hard, but she didn't have Miranda's intellectual edge. Miranda was her sister, two years older, and already at Oxford.

So Mr. and Mrs. Buchan greeted Imogen's tentative suggestion that she should go in for nurse training with enthusiasm. She obviously had a *vocation*, they said. Of course they would respect her decision. And that was the line they took with friends. They thought Imogen was *so* brave not to opt automatically for university, they told the stream of dinner-party guests who came to the house that summer. They knew she had a lot to give. Imogen, who hated the gatherings where the talk was of novels she had never read and of the philistine horrors of the National Curriculum, would blush awkwardly and turn away.

Now Imogen was twenty-two and qualified, quite competent to take charge of a ward. More competent, her colleagues often agreed, than some sisters they could mention.

She found in nursing something at which she could excel. At last she had her own field of interest and her parents could stop comparing her unfavourably with Miranda. Imogen had such a sense of responsibility! they said. Such dedication!

Despite this, Imogen was vaguely conscious that during her training there had been an element of competition with her sister, all the more humiliating because Miranda was unaware of it and spent her time at university in a sleepless round of parties and political activity. Imogen had been so determined to succeed that before she was qualified, her social life had been nonexistent.

Her time off was spent at home, writing up her patient studies, preparing the next essay. With the other students she was shy, embarrassed. In those three years she had never had a real boyfriend, and their casual talk of affairs and separations made her feel inadequate. They put her quietness down to snobbishness. She sensed their hostility and grew even more reserved.

Yet on the ward, especially with the elderly or the very ill, she blossomed. The patients seemed unintimidated by her, more comfortable when she was there. The other students came to resent her skill. When they had all qualified, there was less pressure to do well and she had more confidence. She would have welcomed then the opportunity to go out with them, but they had stopped asking.

She had met Patrick through her parents at one of the dreadful dinner parties the autumn after she qualified. He was just about to start at the university. Ann Buchan had joined a support group set up by Dorothea to provide funds for the orphanage where she had worked in Africa, and an improbable friendship had developed. In Imogen's view the women had nothing in common. Her mother had a middle-class tolerance to every point of view, except conventional Christianity, which she dismissed, quite categorically, as superstition. Yet she seemed to admire Dorothea immensely and the Cassidys became regulars at the house. On this occasion Patrick had been invited, too, probably, Imogen suspected, to provide company for her, as if she were a child and unable to follow the adult conversation. Miranda had disappeared early back to Oxford, claiming that Northumberland bored her.

It was mid-September and it had been raining steadily all day, so when the Cassidys arrived, they would have to run up the path under dripping trees. When the doorbell rang, Mrs. Buchan was still upstairs, not quite ready for them.

"Open the door, darling," she shouted down to Imogen. "And get everyone a drink."

But a drink of what? Imogen wondered with horror. If they wanted wine, it would be impossible. She had never once opened a bottle without leaving shreds of cork floating on the top. And she never knew exactly how much to give.

Yet when she opened the door, Patrick stood there alone, as obviously unhappy about the dinner party as she was. Could they borrow an umbrella? he asked grudgingly. Edward and Dorothea were still in the car and had forgotten theirs. Outside, it was dark and he stood under the porch light, his hair plastered against his forehead, very tall. She wanted to reach out and touch his wet jacket and kiss his wet hair. Her stomach dipped and her head spun. It was the first time she had felt such a physical attraction. So this is what it's all about? she thought, astonished. All that gossiping and giggling in corners. I never realised. She found two umbrellas and walked with him down the path to the car.

"There's no need to come out," he said, but she thought he was glad she was there. They took an umbrella each and walked in single file up the path, kept apart by the spokes. Then they gave one to Edward and Dorothea and shared the other. The Cassidys ran off, laughing, toward the house, splashing in the puddles on the muddy path. Patrick and

125

Imogen followed slowly and he put his arm around her waist to hold her in out of the rain.

"Isn't he a bit young for you, darling?" her mother had said when she started going out with him. "He's only eighteen. Only a boy. We were rather hoping you would find a nice doctor."

That was only half a joke. Doctors were graduates with a high status and a good income. But she accepted Patrick as second best as she had accepted nursing. He would be a graduate, too, one day and there was something charmingly old-fashioned about being the son of a clergyman. Mrs. Buchan told her friends that age was irrelevant these days and Patrick was so mature for an eighteen-year-old.

"Perhaps," she would say, hopefully, "he will introduce Imogen to some culture."

And occasionally she would question her daughter after an evening out with Patrick.

"Where did he take you, darling? Did you see that new thing at the Playhouse?"

"No," Imogen would say vaguely. "We were out with friends, for a meal, you know. . . ."

But that was a lie. She would have considered time in the theatre or a restaurant as wasted. Patrick had a friend with a room in one of the halls of residence and usually they went there to make love. At other times they walked, for miles, along small country roads, or they sat by the river and talked. In the beginning they never squandered their time together by sharing it with other young people.

A different mother might have been concerned about her daughter. Imogen became so wrapped up in her infatuation for Patrick that she lost all her other interests. She lost touch with the few friends she had kept from school. When she was not a work, she thought of nothing else. If there was a day when he could not see her, she brooded, imagining some secret betrayal. Nothing mattered so much as their relationship. She found it difficult to sleep. She stopped eating regularly and grew thin, paler than ever. The weight loss suited her and gave her a luminous, insubstantial quality, but she seemed always tired.

If her mother noticed the change in Imogen, it did not worry her. She was in love. What could be more natural? Ann Buchan was busy with the preparation for exams, her voluntary work, with entertaining. Imogen worked shifts and spent every hour she could with Patrick. The two hardly ever met. It was Miranda, home for a long weekend to sleep off the effects of a particularly hectic term, who said:

"Bloody hell, Imo, what have you been doing? You look positively anorexic."

Still, Ann Buchan was not concerned. Eating disorders happened to silly sixteen-year-olds, not mature nurses. Work on the cancer ward was particularly stressful and Imogen was tired, that was all. She met Imogen one night in the kitchen as her daughter was heating up a bowl of soup in the microwave and made what she thought was a helpful suggestion:

"We hardly ever see you now, darling. Have you ever thought of moving in with Patrick? Get a flat perhaps in town. It would be less tiring for you both and we might see more of you on your days off."

Ann Buchan was proud of herself. She thought it broadminded to have suggested that arrangement, but to her surprise Imogen did not reply. She stared at her mother in silent resentment and went to her room, leaving the soup uneaten.

That conversation with her mother came back to Imogen as she drove along the winding road which led to Otterbridge. It was half-past two. She switched on the radio, but the local news was all about the murder of Dorothea Cassidy and she switched it off again, quickly, trying to pretend that the tragedy had never happened.

12

Hilary Masters, the social worker, dropped Stephen Ramsay at the police station at half-past two. The catch on the passenger door was stuck and she had to lean across him to release it. Her fingers were trembling and she remained with her arm across his chest, fiddling with the handle for some time. It was a knack, she said, when at last it opened. She laughed but she seemed flustered. Their closeness, as she stretched to reach the door, seemed to have disturbed them both.

What about a meal when this is all over? he wanted to say. We've more in common than you realise.

He sensed her loneliness and it pleased him to think he might help her. For the first time since Diana had left him, he felt the possibility of committing himself to a relationship. The women had nothing in common. Diana was dark, impulsive, with a furious temper. Yet he was curious about Hilary in the same way as in the beginning he had been curious about Diana. That was the attraction. But he could not find the courage to make the invitation. By then the door was open and she was upright, as poised as ever, staring in front of her as if to suggest that she was a busy woman and he had already taken up too much of her time.

Hunter was in the canteen, sadly eating a yoghurt. Since

he had begun training for the Great North Run he had taken to choosing healthy foods—salad, fruit, the cranky vegetarian dishes which the canteen staff occasionally prepared and which were always left over at the end of the day—but he had never enjoyed them. Now, after the trip to the hospital, he felt he deserved something more substantial. His failure to discover what Dorothea Cassidy had been doing there hurt his pride. Worse, he had to listen to Annie Ramsay in the backseat telling Emily Bowman what a brilliant man her nephew was.

"He was brainy even as a bairn," she had said. "The first in our family to get to the grammar. Eh, Emily, you should have seen him the first day in his uniform. Little grey shorts and a cherry-red cap and blazer." Then she had called across, "Did you go to the grammar, Mr. Hunter?"

He said that in his day it was all comprehensive, but she sniffed disdainfully as if that made no difference to anything. Stephen was a clever man, she said, and Mr. Hunter was lucky to work on his team. It was almost more than the policeman could bear.

Hunter stood up and ordered a sausage sandwich, joking with the woman behind the counter as he waited to be served. He took it back to his table just as Ramsay came into the room.

"Five minutes," Ramsay said. "In my office."

Hunter nodded. He pressed the bread of his sandwich together so the grease dripped through and bit into it hungrily. Ramsay chose black coffee and a cheese roll then disappeared. Hunter finished the sandwich, wiped his hands on a paper napkin, and followed him.

"Well?" Hunter said, leaning against the door frame of the inspector's office. "How did you get on with your social worker?" He spoke as if social workers, like mothers-in-law, were inevitably a source of humour.

I don't know how I get on with her, Ramsay thought. How can you tell what a woman is thinking about?

He drank coffee and kept his voice cool. "I think we have a possible suspect," he said. "His name's Corkhill, Joss Corkhill. Does the name mean anything to you?"

Hunter shook his head. Ramsay pushed a computer printout of the man's record across the table towards him.

"Dorothea Cassidy was at a social services case conference yesterday morning. It was to decide whether or not a child should be taken into care. Dorothea had discovered that the girl was probably being battered by the mother's boyfriend—that's Corkhill. He's working on the fair at the meadow and wants to move on when it packs up—with the mother. Dorothea tried to persuade her to stay here with her kids. Corkhill's a boozer with a pretty violent temper. He was expected back at the house this lunchtime, but he didn't turn up."

Hunter nodded, impressed but unwilling to give Ramsay any credit for the discovery.

"Where's Corkhill now?"

Ramsay shrugged. "He was at the fair this morning. I've put out a general alert. He'll not have got far."

"So it's all over," Hunter said. It was the sort of case he could understand after all. A man with too many beers inside him losing his temper with an interfering busybody of a woman.

"I don't know. . . ." Ramsay said. "There's a coincidence. The family is called Stringer and there's a boy, a halfbrother of the child who's been taken into care, who works at Armstrong House."

"Is that important?"

Ramsay shrugged again.

"Dorothea was there visiting yesterday afternoon and she was supposed to be giving a talk to the old people in the evening," he said. "It might be relevant."

130

"Have we got a time of death yet?" In the past Hunter had dismissed Ramsay's doubts as a form of cowardice, but Ramsay had been right too often for an ambitious man like the sergeant to ignore him.

"Provisional," Ramsay said. "Between ten and midnight."

"But I thought she was reported missing early in the evening."

"She was," Ramsay said. It was the thing that was troubling him most. "I wish I knew what happened to her after she left the Stringers at quarter past five."

"Perhaps she was abducted," Hunter said. "Kept alive against her will. Was there any sexual assault?"

Ramsay shook his head.

"What's the theory then?" Hunter said. "Was Corkhill waiting for her when she came out of Theresa's house?"

"I don't think so," Ramsay said. "She had a car. He didn't. If he'd approached her between the house and the car, someone would have noticed. Perhaps he was waiting for her at Armstrong House. He had an excuse for being there through Clive."

"I think I saw the boy hanging round there this morning," Hunter said. "A vacant-looking lad . . ."

Ramsay nodded. "Clive Stringer can drive," he said. "He's no licence, but he's been done for taking and driving away several times. Perhaps Corkhill used him to get rid of the car. He was out last night. He claims to have been at the fair, but that's no sort of alibi. He's simple and might have chosen to leave it close to where he works, just because it was familiar."

"It would tie in with the evidence of the only witness I could find in Tanner's street," Hunter said. "He claims to have seen the car being badly driven all over the road. That might mean an inexperienced driver."

"The lad won't be easy to interview," Ramsay said, "I've

131

had one go at him. He's frightened of something. Perhaps I'll ask the social worker to talk to him. She might get more out of him than me."

Was that an excuse? he wondered suddenly, a means of seeing Hilary Masters again.

"At least we can work out a timetable of Mrs. Cassidy's movements well into the afternoon," he said briskly, putting all thoughts of the immaculate Miss Masters from his mind. "What time did she leave Emily Bowman?"

"At about half-past three," Hunter said, "after she'd taken Mrs. Bowman to Newcastle General Hospital for her X-ray treatment." He explained that there was someone in the hospital Dorothea wanted to see.

"I've arranged for some publicity on the wards and the outpatient department," he said, "but there's been no response yet. I spoke to a staff nurse—Imogen Buchan. She was there all yesterday afternoon, but she didn't see Mrs. Cassidy."

Ramsay looked up from the notes he was taking. The name was unusual but strangely familiar. He thought he had heard it recently, but could not place it. He worried at it for a moment then gave up.

"Was Mrs. Bowman definite about the time?" he asked. "Clive Stringer claims that Dorothea went into Mrs. Bowman's room and was still there at four o'clock."

"He must have made a mistake," Hunter said. "Or he's lying. She didn't go into Mrs. Bowman's flat when they got back from the hospital. According to the old lady, Mrs. Cassidy helped her into the lift then left. She was in a hurry, Mrs. Bowman said, and only took her to the lift because everyone else was playing bingo and there was no one to help."

It seemed impossible to Ramsay that Clive should have made a mistake. He had been so insistent about the time. Why then would he want to lie?

"What now?" Hunter asked. He was like a small boy whose attention wanders easily. All the talk made him restless.

Ramsay stood up and walked to the window. He could see the old town walls, which had been built to keep out the marauding Scots, and the crowds already starting to gather for the evening's parade. He opened the window and there was the faint sound of fairground music. Some of the smaller rides must have already started.

"We have to know where Dorothea Cassidy was yesterday evening," he said. "She can't have vanished without trace."

Yet, he thought, looking down at the crowd, there were so many people in Otterbridge during festival week, that it might be possible to disappear into them.

He was going to give Hunter more detailed instructions when the phone on his desk began to ring, and then immediately afterwards the phone on Hunter's desk in the adjoining room. The two calls must have come through to the switchboard within seconds of each other. Later Ramsay checked and found that they were both logged for four o'clock.

Hunter took the call that came into his room. It was from a policeman who had picked up Joss Corkhill.

"Tell your boss I want a medal for this," the man said breathlessly. "His bloody dog bit my leg."

"Where are you?" Hunter asked.

"On the bypass close to the Ridgeway Estate."

Ramsay received the news that Clive Stringer was dead.

His first reaction was a sense of failure. He had botched the Corkhill arrest and should have realised that the boy was vulnerable. He had decided, after all, that Clive was probably Corkhill's accomplice. He was quite certain, at first, that the boy's death confirmed Corkhill's guilt. When Hunter came bounding back into the office with the news that Corkhill had been picked up, he thought the thing was all over.

Then more details came in and Ramsay's certainty turned to panic. He learned with horror that Walter Tanner's house had been used for the second murder. There was no suggestion that Corkhill had ever met Tanner, let alone that he had a reason for wanting to implicate the churchwarden in Clive's death. Tanner had become an obvious suspect.

Hunter wanted to be at the scene of the crime. He bounced impatiently from one foot to the other like a runner at the start of a race. Ramsay knew his mind would already be racing in tabloid headlines.

"Well?" Hunter demanded. "Are you coming?"

Ramsay shook his head. "Not yet. You go. Take charge. See what you can get out of the old man."

Delighted, Hunter ran off, jumping down stairs three at a time, slamming doors, making as much of a drama as he could manage. Ramsay sat quietly at his desk waiting for information.

It came relentlessly, proving conclusively that Corkhill could have played no active part in Clive's murder. The arresting officer reported that Corkhill had been standing on the bypass for at least an hour waiting for a lift. He was drunk and disreputable and no one had stopped. He had been seen by a number of council workmen who were digging up that stretch of road. Then the pathologist who arrived promptly at Tanner's house to examine the body said that Clive was only recently dead. He had died perhaps only a matter of minutes before Tanner found him, he told Ramsay cheerfully over the telephone. Certainly not more than half an hour. So Ramsay realised that unless there was the coincidence of two murderers in Otterbridge, each separately choosing to implicate Walter Tanner, Corkhill had not killed Dorothea Cassidy. Ramsay ordered more black coffee and knew he would have to start from the beginning again.

From his office he made several phone calls. The first was to Hilary Masters.

"Hold the line a minute," the receptionist said, "while I check that she's in."

Then there was the social worker's voice, cool and professional, matching the formality of his own. He told her, unemotionally, that Clive Stringer was dead and there was a silence. He wondered even if she had been called away from the phone, but when at last she answered, it was obvious that she had been crying.

"I'm sorry," she said. "I was fond of him."

He was terribly moved but could think of nothing to say to comfort her.

"I've sent a WPC to tell Theresa," he said, "but I thought you would want to visit."

"Yes," she said. "Of course."

There was a silence. "Who killed him?" she cried suddenly. "Was it Joss?"

"No," he said. "We've brought Mr. Corkhill to help us with our enquiries, but it's unlikely that he'll be charged."

He realised he was hiding behind the jargon. He did not know how to respond to her distress.

"Then who was it?" she cried again.

"We don't know," he said. "Not yet." He had never felt so inadequate.

"Will you be coming to talk to Theresa today?" she said. "Will I see you there?"

"I won't be there until later," he said. "I know you're very busy. Perhaps you won't have the time to wait."

"Don't worry," she said. "I'll wait. I think I should be there when you talk to Theresa. Besides . . ."

Her voice trailed off and yet he was left with the sense that a promise had been made, that the possibility of contact between them had been established, and he was excited as a boy.

The next phone call was made to the Walkers. His determination that he should start again at the beginning made the

135

Cassidys an obvious target of investigation. When the phone rang, Dolly was picking raspberries, stooping under the nets which were supposed to stop the birds taking the fruit, and she heard the bell through the open kitchen door. It took some time for her to disentangle herself from the net and she expected the phone to stop before she reached it, but it continued with a persistence which frightened her. When she picked up the receiver, her hand was shaking.

"Yes?" she said. "Hello?" She expected it to be her husband.

"Mrs. Walker," Ramsay said. "I wonder if I might speak to Edward Cassidy."

She felt defensive, as if he had accused her of neglecting her duty.

"He's not here," she said, and felt herself blushing. "He insisted on going home. We tried to persuade him, but he wasn't himself at all."

"Patrick then? It is rather urgent."

"No," she said. "Patrick is not here either. We were rather worried about Patrick. He went off in such a state. Actually my husband's out looking for him." Then she stopped abruptly, feeling strangely disloyal.

Ramsay probed gently for precise times—when exactly had Patrick left them? he asked. What time did they leave the vicar in Otterbridge?

She sensed that something was wrong and became flustered and evasive. She was no good about time, she said. Ramsay would have to talk to her husband. But when the major returned from his unsuccessful attempt to find Patrick, he persuaded her that it was dangerous to lie and that the police had their own methods to get to the truth. He saw it might be safer to distance themselves from the Cassidys.

13

Ramsay was tempted to leave Joss Corkhill to be interviewed by someone else. It seemed now that the man was only on the periphery of the investigation, an incidental distraction. Let Hilary Masters sort out the Stringer family's problems. Yet Joss had a reason to seek out Dorothea Cassidy on the afternoon of her death. And Ramsay was curious to meet the man who had brought such apparent joy to Theresa Stringer's life and who had betrayed her trust so completely. Later Ramsay was glad that he had taken the time to talk to Corkhill. The conversation gave him the first glimmer of a real motive.

After the hours of waiting, Corkhill was sober and looked ill and drained like all alcoholics needing a drink. He was perfectly at home in the interview room. He sat with his elbows on the table and his head in his hands, his eyes shut, and though he must have heard Ramsay come into the room, he did not move. He was a slight man with dark, curly hair, and the inspector could see why Theresa might have found him attractive. He had cultivated the image of the travelling man. He was dressed in a striped collarless shirt, the sort students had worn when Ramsay was young, and a grey waistcoat. Round his neck was tied a red cotton scarf. In the interview he was almost entirely self-centred, yet occasionally there were bursts of wit and self-mockery. When he had had a drink or two, Ramsay could see that he would be good company, lively, funny, but wanting always to be the centre of attraction.

He opened his eyes, though still he did not look at Ramsay. He spoke with a thick Merseyside accent.

"What have you done with my dog?" he said. "That's a valuable animal. I'll not have her ill-treated. She might be sick already, poisoned. She took a good bite out of that pig's leg."

Ramsay said nothing. It was as if Corkhill had never spoken. He sat at the table and arranged paper in front of him, a fussy civil servant, then switched on the tape recorder to begin the interview.

"We have a problem, Mr. Corkhill," he said in his polite, civil servant's voice, "and we think you may be able to help us. Perhaps you would be kind enough to answer a few questions."

Corkhill looked up. "What *is* this all about?" he said.

"Come now, Mr. Corkhill," Ramsay said. "I'm sure you know. I would have thought that the news of Mrs. Cassidy's murder must have reached the Ridgeway by now. A major talking point, I should have thought, the murder of a vicar's wife in a town like Otterbridge."

Corkhill shrugged. "Nothing to do with me, pal," he said.

"But you did know Mrs. Cassidy?" Ramsay persisted.

"So did most of Otterbridge," Corkhill said. "She had her nose into everything."

"But recently I understand you came under her special attention."

Corkhill refused to answer directly. "Look," he said. "This is intimidation. Why pick on me? I know you haven't locked away the old boy who had her car on his drive. I saw him today."

"Do you know Mr. Tanner?" he asked.

138

Corkhill smiled, aware that his ploy to distract Ramsay had succeeded.

"I've met him a few times," he said airily. He paused for dramatic effect. "Usually in the bookies on the Ridgeway. He's a regular there. Always loses. Didn't you know? Not much of a detective, are you? I saw him there today."

Ramsay wrote a brief note but gave Corkhill the satisfaction of no further response.

"To return to Mrs. Cassidy," he said. "You didn't like her very much, did you, Mr. Corkhill. She interfered in your private life and I suspect that you rather resented it."

"Not at first," Corkhill said. "At first I thought she was all right. On our side."

"But later you came to resent her?" Ramsay persisted.

Corkhill was finding it increasingly difficult to maintain the pose of flippancy. He needed a drink, and the soft, insinuating questions had begun to irritate him. His uncertainty made him want to lash out.

"She was an interfering cow!" he said. "Theresa and me had everything arranged. We were going to work together, a team, like the real Gypsies. Then Mrs. bloody Cassidy stuck her nose in and spoilt it. You don't know what she was like. . . ."

"No," Ramsay said. "Well . . . perhaps you had better tell me. Did you meet her at Miss Stringer's house?"

"There was no bloody avoiding it once she took on the lad," Corkhill said. "I thought she understood me. She'd travelled herself. We talked. Then she found a few bruises on the kid and everything changed. She came to the house, all high and mighty, laying down the law. 'I think this is a family problem, don't you? And you're part of the family, Mr. Corkhill.' " He spoke in a falsetto parody of a woman's voice. "She was so bloody sure of herself," he went on. "And so bloody sure she knew what was best for us all."

"It's a responsibility taking on a woman with two kids," Ramsay said. "How did you get on with Clive?"

Corkhill shrugged. "He's all right," he said. "Not very bright, but then brains don't run in the family."

"What about Beverley?" Ramsay asked. "Is she a backward child?"

"No," Corkhill said grudgingly. "She's got more about her than her brother."

"That must have been very demanding," Ramsay said. "I understand that bright children are often demanding."

"Look," Corkhill said, confiding, world-weary. "I know what this is all about. I had it all out with that Mrs. Cassidy. 'Why do you blame everything on me?' I told her. 'How do you know it wasn't Theresa who knocked the kid around. She lost a baby before after all.' "

"But it wasn't Theresa who knocked Beverley around," Ramsay said. "Was it? Theresa told us what happened. And she told Mrs. Cassidy yesterday. Mrs. Cassidy wanted to talk to you about it. And she persuaded Theresa that she couldn't go away with you. You wouldn't like that."

Corkhill longed for a drink. His attention was wandering and he could think of nothing else. He moved restlessly in his seat. Ramsay noted his discomfort.

"Now I want to talk about yesterday," the inspector said. "Perhaps you could give me an account of your movements. You worked on the fair in the morning?"

Corkhill nodded.

"What time did you get back to Miss Stringer's house?"

"Two o'clock. Half-past." He wanted the interview to be over so he could get out.

"What did you and Theresa talk about?"

"Nothing!" Corkhill said defensively. "I wanted some peace before I started work again. What would there be to talk about?"

140

"Her daughter had been taken into care," Ramsay said. "She might have thought that worth a mention."

The sarcasm was lost on Corkhill.

"Oh that!" he said. "She was rambling on about that, but I told her to shut up."

"I thought you had a row. Didn't Theresa tell you she wasn't going to come away with you after all?"

This surprised Corkhill. He hadn't expected Ramsay to have so much detailed information about him.

"You were angry, weren't you?" Ramsay went on. "You thought Theresa had let you down. And you blamed Dorothea Cassidy. She came back later to talk to Theresa. Did you wait to have it out with her?"

"No!" Corkhill said. "I didn't touch her. I didn't even see her then. I was bloody angry and I went out to work."

"What time was that?"

"About four o'clock."

"What happened then?" Ramsay asked. "How did you get into town?"

"I walked. I've not got money to spend on bus fares."

"Did you stop anywhere on the way?"

Corkhill hesitated. "I needed a drink," he said. "I stopped at the off-licence on the estate."

"Did you see Dorothea's car on its way to the Ridgeway?"

Corkhill shook his head. "I was bloody angry," he said. "I didn't see anything."

"What time did you get to the fair?"

"Half-past four," Corkhill said. "Quarter to five. And I was there all evening. My mate will tell you."

"You didn't slip away to the pub? For a meal?"

"It was too busy," he said. "We had some chips on the site."

That's it then, Ramsay thought. It's impossible for him to have killed Dorothea Cassidy. Even without the news of Clive's death, they would have to let him go. He was preparing to tell Corkhill that the boy was dead when Corkhill volunteered information of his own.

"She was there last night," he said. "At the fair. She didn't come to my ride, but I saw her all the same."

"Who?" Ramsay demanded. "Who was there?"

"The vicar's wife. Mrs. Cassidy." He spoke as if Ramsay was a fool.

"Are you sure?"

"Of course I'm sure. She was wearing that blue jacket. I'd know her anywhere."

"Did you talk to her?"

"No," Corkhill said, reluctantly, as if admitting some lack of courage. "By then I'd calmed down again. It didn't seem worth making a fuss."

"What time did you see her?"

He shrugged. "I don't know. It wasn't late. Sometime between eight and half-past."

"Was she on her own?"

"No," Corkhill said. Despite himself he was enjoying the sense of importance the information was giving him. He could tell Ramsay was excited. He paused, tantalising the inspector, smiling.

"Well?" Ramsay said. "Who was with her?"

"It was a woman," Corkhill said. "A pale thing, pretty enough."

"What were they doing?"

"How should I know?" Corkhill said. "I was busy. There was a crowd."

"But you must have seen something."

"They were walking together, talking. There's nothing else to say."

Ramsay was already planning the next stage of the investigation. They would put as many men as he could spare into the fair that night, with photographs of Dorothea. Who was the woman with her? Corkhill's description had stirred some vague memory. Perhaps Cassidy would know, he thought.

"Can I go then?" Corkhill said, suddenly cocky.

"Not yet," Ramsay said. "I'm afraid I have some news for you." He spoke in exactly the same tone as before. "Clive Stringer is dead. He was found murdered this afternoon."

He watched the man carefully and was convinced it came as a surprise to him.

"I didn't know," Corkhill said. Then, with a burst of temper: "I suppose you want to pin that on me, too."

Ramsay shook his head.

"Just make a statement," he said. "Then you can go. I expect Theresa will be glad of your support at a time like this."

Corkhill shook his head. "No," he said. "I've had enough. I'm not going back there. She's too much like bloody trouble. I'm going back on the road. On my own."

He stared out of the window.

Ramsay stood up to leave the room when Corkhill spoke again.

"Poor bastard," he said. "He didn't have much of a life, did he?"

It seemed a fitting epitaph for the boy.

As Ramsay got to his office the phone was ringing.

"It's your aunt," someone said. "She says it's urgent."

Ramsay almost refused to speak to her. Tell her I'm too busy, he wanted to say. She can leave a message. But the conversation with Corkhill had chilled him. Corkhill had lost the habit of human contact. He cared for Theresa but preferred loneliness to the responsibilities that came through living with her. Perhaps I'm like that, Ramsay thought. I resent the demands of friendship. So when Annie came through to him, he spoke to her kindly, with unusual warmth. But he knew it was all pretence and like Corkhill he was better on his own.

* * *

In Armstrong House Annie Ramsay had been playing detectives. At lunchtime she had cancelled the afternoon's bingo. It wasn't fitting, she said, after such a tragedy. All the same it brought everyone together for a laugh and a cup of tea and she missed it.

When she first got back from the hospital she pottered around her flat, making scones, thinking that later she would take them round to Emily's so they could share some tea. She wasn't much of a cook. Not like her mother . . . With the memory of her mother, the warm kitchen, the big range in the pit cottage where she had grown up, she pulled herself together. She had always vowed that she would never become one of those old people who bored the pants off the world by talking about when they were bairns. There was more to life than dreaming about the past. Her flat was too quiet, that was the trouble. It looked over the respectable street leading to the park, and at this time in the afternoon the children were at school and the parents were away to their offices in the town. She wanted a bit of bustle, a bit of something to watch.

At the front of the building there was a small patch of garden—some lawn, a few pots of geraniums, and a wooden bench donated, according to the plaque on the back, by St. Mary's Mothers' Union. The bench was seldom used—too bloody uncomfortable for one thing, Annie thought as she settled herself onto it. And too close to the busy road with its noise, fumes, and dust. From where she sat she could see the main road into town and round the corner into Armstrong Street. There, in the midafternoon heat, everything seemed quiet, lifeless. In one of the gardens was a pram with a dazzling white sunshade, but throughout the afternoon the baby made no sound. A little way up the street a car was started. It pulled into the street and disappeared over the brow of the hill into shadow. Annie was aware of it because it was the

144

first thing to move in the street since she had been sitting there, but later she was unable to describe it at all.

"What about the colour?" Ramsay would say impatiently when she phoned him. "You must have seen that."

But she had to tell the truth and say she had no idea. She was able, however, to give him an accurate time, because as the car drove off, the bell in the primary school on the main street was rung and the children ran out to the lollipop lady on the zebra crossing. The schoolday finished at quarter to four.

She spent a few minutes looking at the children, trying to recognise the ones who lived locally, delighting in how brown and healthy they were. When she looked back into Armstrong Street, she saw Walter Tanner walking from the direction toward which the car had driven. She had never liked Walter Tanner—his mother had gone to school with Annie and she had always found her a snooty cow—but as she watched him walk slowly along the street she was moved to pity.

"It was as if he had all the cares of the world on his shoulders," she would tell Ramsay later.

"But the time? What time did Mr. Tanner get home?"

"Ten to four," she would say, quite certain, tempted for a moment to lie, just to please him.

"Are you sure that it couldn't have been earlier?"

And she would shake her head, disappointed and frustrated because she couldn't be of more help.

She watched Walter Tanner shuffle down the street to his front door and pause there as if he needed to collect his breath. She saw him take out his keys, then push open the door, surprised at not needing them. She missed the arrival of the ambulance, Gordon Hunter, and the pathologist because she had decided by then that detecting might run in the family and she could do some investigating of her own.

It had occurred to her while she was sitting in the sun that

145

Thursday was when the church was cleaned. There was a duty roster. Annie took her turn with the other ladies to polish pews, Hoover the floor, and do the silver. Dorothea had tried to persuade some men to be involved in these domestic chores, but they had been surprisingly resistant. So, someone would have been in the church the evening before. The Hoover, the dusters, and the polish were kept in the scullery next to the vicarage kitchen. If Dorothea had returned to the vicarage after all, it was possible that one of the cleaning ladies had seen her.

Annie Ramsay found the rota in the drawer of her kitchen table. The first two names against June 20th were of no interest to her. They were active pensioners, keen bowlers, who did their cleaning early in the morning to leave the rest of the day free for their sport. The third was more hopeful. She went under the improbable name of Cuthbertina David and she lived in a flat in Armstrong House.

Cuthbertina David was a tall, angular woman with wild, white hair and enormous flat feet. She was deaf and her hearing aid seemed little use to her. Annie Ramsay stood in the corridor and knocked on Cuthbertina's door. She was very excited. There was no answer. She knocked again, growing more and more impatient and frustrated. She knew Cuthbertina was there. If the deaf old bat didn't come soon, she would have to fetch the warden for her key. At last the door opened.

"Eh, I'm sorry, hinnie," the woman said. In contrast to her manic appearance her voice was soft and melodic. "I didn't hear you. Come in."

"I've come about Mrs. Cassidy," Annie yelled. "You must have heard about the tragedy."

"No, hinnie. What tragedy's that?"

"Didn't the police come to talk to you this morning?"

"I've been in all morning and I've seen no one. But maybe they knocked and I didn't hear the door."

146

Annie shouted an explanation of what had happened, then came to the point.

"It was your day for church cleaning yesterday," she said.

"Aye," Cuthbertina said. "I can't do any heavy work now. Not with the arthritis so bad. But they let me do the silver. I can sit to do that."

"Did you have to go to the vicarage?"

"Of course. Like I always do. Even if they're all out, there's a key to the backdoor in the vestry."

"Were they all out yesterday?"

"No. I thought some would be there because Mrs. Cassidy's car was parked in the drive."

"Did you see Mrs. Cassidy?"

"Yes. She was in the kitchen with the lad, Patrick. I thought she might give me a cup of tea. She'd just made a brew, but they seemed to be busy, serious, you know. I don't think the lad saw me even, he was that engrossed."

"What were they talking about?"

"Eh, hinnie, you know what my hearing's like. I didn't go into the kitchen, only the scullery. How could I tell?"

"What was the time?" Annie Ramsay said. "Do you know what the time was when you saw her in the vicarage?"

"Aye," Cuthbertina said. "It was half-past five. I looked up at the church clock."

"Did you go back later to take the cleaning stuff?"

"No," Cuthbertina said. "I thought I'd leave it in the vestry just this once. I got the idea Mrs. Cassidy wouldn't want to be disturbed."

Triumphantly Annie Ramsay scuttled back to her flat to phone her nephew to tell him the news and receive his admiration.

14

When Imogen arrived in Otterbridge, she drove straight to the vicarage. Edward Cassidy had the kitchen door open before she could get out of the car and walked out onto the square patch of gravel at the side of the house, shielding his eyes from the bright sunlight with one hand, to see who it was. She could tell at once that he was disappointed, and they stared at each other, not sure what to say. He was so grey and confused that Imogen wondered if he might be physically ill.

"I was looking for Patrick," she said at last. "I wanted to help. I don't know. . . ."

He shook his head.

"He's not here," he said. "I don't know where he went." Then plaintively: "He's taken my car."

"How is he?" she asked.

"Upset," he said. "Dreadfully upset. He was very fond of his stepmother."

Oh yes, Imogen thought bitterly. We all know how fond he was of Dorothea.

He tried to persuade her to go into the house with him, to take some tea, share the burden of waiting for Patrick, but she refused to go. She knew Edward wanted to talk about Dorothea and she could not stand that. She almost ran back to her car and drove away too quickly, so that the wheels spun on the gravel and the cats which had been sleeping on the back doorstep in the sun slid silently away into the house.

She drove through the town to her parents' house. She thought Patrick might try to get in touch with her there. The progress through the crowded streets was slow and she swore to herself and hit the horn with her fist when pedestrians would not move out of her way. In the square by the almshouses some sort of pageant was in progress. It was full of children in mediaeval dress. Bloody festival, she thought. The whole town goes mad at this time of the year.

Her parents lived in a large semidetached villa in one of the quiet streets close to the park. She had long since stopped thinking of it as her home, though she had never lived anywhere else, except in a nurses' home for the first few months of her training. And she'd hated that. All along the street, in the gardens and by the side of the road, trees were in blossom. Much of it was past its best, so the pavement and parked cars and tidy front lawns were covered with the shrivelled pink flowers. Her mother laughed at the neighbours' attempts to sweep the dead blossoms away. "What does it matter?" she would say. "There'll only be more tomorrow. What tedious lives those people must live if they can think of nothing better to do."

I expect she considers I lead a tedious life, Imogen thought.

She pulled her car onto the pavement, leaving the drive free for her parents' Volvo and walked down the long, narrow garden to the house. Just inside the door was a pile of post and she stopped to pick it up, absently looking through the envelopes to see if there was anything for her. There was one letter. It was in a cheap white envelope and the address was written in a handwriting she did not recognise. She took it with her to the kitchen and put it on the table while she filled a kettle to make coffee. All the time she was willing the phone to ring, or the doorbell. Patrick would have an

149

explanation for everything, she thought. If only Patrick turned up, everything would be all right. She made instant coffee in a mug with a cartoon of Margaret Thatcher on the side and opened the letter.

Dear Imogen, it said. *I'm sorry you were so upset today. I think we should meet when I've more time. We need to talk. Perhaps we could have a meal together. I'm sure you've no reason to worry. I'll be in touch soon.*

It was written in a bold and confident hand and it was signed *Dorothea*. Imogen could imagine her writing it, dashing it off in a moment, perhaps while she was sitting in her car outside some client's house. There was nothing new in the letter. It was a gesture, a form of showing off. Look at me, it said. I'm incredibly busy but I can still find time to show my stepson's neurotic girlfriend that I care about her. It was as if she had seen a ghost. She tore the letter into pieces, then set fire to the paper in an ashtray. She rinsed the mug and the ashtray under the tap and went up the stairs to her room.

She had first suspected that Patrick was in love with Dorothea Cassidy on Easter Sunday. She remembered it vividly. She had been invited to the vicarage for lunch, then she and Patrick had spent the afternoon together, walking along the River Otter. There was a quiet, overgrown place where they knew they would not be disturbed. They lay under the trees and threw stones into the water. She had her head on his stomach and he stroked the hair away from her face.

"We should elope," he had said, "and live here forever."

She had moved away from him, so she was facedown, watching the dragonflies on the river. She did not look at him because she was nervous about what he might say. "Why don't you leave the vicarage?" she asked. "Perhaps we could get a flat together."

"Perhaps we could!" he said, apparently enthusiastic, so she rolled back onto her side and took his hand, relieved.

150

But when she went on to make real plans, to discuss where they might live, when he might move, he said it was not something to hurry.

"There's plenty of time," he said, expansively. "We're all right as we are."

So she realised that something was holding him at the vicarage. She thought at first it might be his affection for his father. They had been alone for such a long time that there must be a special bond. It was only later on that Easter Sunday as they were walking back in the dusk through the trees with the sound of church bells in the distance, that Patrick made some casual reference to his stepmother. The trivial remark was made with such reverence that she saw, quite suddenly, that the real attraction was Dorothea.

Since then she had considered Dorothea a rival. Even when she was most depressed, she had never dreamt that there was anything physical between them, but in comparison with Dorothea she felt excluded and inadequate. The jealousy crept up on her without her realising what was happening. At the start it was a minor irritant, almost amusing. Didn't Patrick see what a fool he was making of himself? she thought. He was too old surely for a teenage crush. It was all the fault of that crazy boys' school his father had sent him to. But it had steadily become more debilitating, and soon the secret and desperate jealousy became as much a part of her relationship with Patrick as her infatuation.

It was a private obsession. She counted the number of times he mentioned Dorothea in each conversation. She noticed that when Dorothea was alone in the vicarage he made excuses to go home early to see her. Imogen knew that the obsession was destructive. She knew her hostility to Dorothea only increased the likelihood of Patrick leaving her, yet she was unable to stop herself. "Why does Dorothea have to run round doing all that social work?" she would ask, sneering. "Hasn't she got enough to do in the church?

Shouldn't she dress more like a vicar's wife?'' Patrick seemed so wrapped up in admiration for his stepmother that he did not notice the criticism, and was only glad of the opportunity to talk about her. Soon Imogen knew even the most intimate details about her. Dorothea could never have children, he said melodramatically. It was one of the tragedies of her life. That was why she was so committed to social work. She loved all the children she worked with as if they were her own.

Not once since Easter Sunday had Imogen actively blamed Dorothea for what was happening to her. She had too little confidence for that. She blamed herself and grew thinner and more frail and beautiful. She just wanted Dorothea out of the way.

Now she had got what she wanted and there was nothing left but this dreadful panic. She lay on her bed and stared up at the ceiling, at the cracks in the plaster she remembered from childhood illnesses, when fever had made the patterns dance in front of her eyes.

I didn't really want her out of the way, she thought. Not literally. Not like that. She would have been able to handle the situation, she thought. Patrick would have seen sense in the end. She would have come to terms with it, if only Dorothea hadn't decided to meddle, if she had not turned up on the ward with her unendurable compassion and her pretensions to sainthood.

Dorothea had arrived on the ward without warning the afternoon before. She had run up the stairs from the radiotherapy outpatients' waiting room and looked glowing, radiant. It was a quiet time and the other nurses were in the canteen having lunch. Imogen was on her own in the office. She had looked up from the desk and there was Dorothea, smiling, slightly out of breath.

"I'm worried about you," Dorothea had said, coming straight to the point. There was never any small talk with

152

Dorothea. She despised it. "You haven't been looking well lately. I never get a chance to see you on your own at the vicarage. Patrick keeps you all to himself."

"I'm fine," Imogen had said, looking blankly out of the window.

"Don't be ridiculous," Dorothea had said, and sat down on the visitors' chair, frowning slightly to show her concern. "You've been miserable for months. Look at all the weight you've lost. What's Patrick been doing to upset you? Or is it work?"

And then, despite herself, Imogen had blurted it all out, and Dorothea had listened, fixing Imogen with such a concentrated look that it seemed that nothing in the world mattered more to her than Imogen's happiness. And she had promised to put everything right.

Imogen had gone home from work that night not sure what to expect. She had wanted to believe that Dorothea had a magical power to arrange things, but was afraid that the meeting between them might provoke some crisis. She had shut herself in her bedroom. Her parents were preparing to go out and she could hear them calling to each other between the bathroom and their bedroom about what earrings went best with her mother's dress. Then the doorbell had rung with an unusual ferocity and she had fled down the stairs to answer it. Patrick stood on the doorstep, as he had on the night they met, and he refused to come in.

"I want to talk to you," he said.

"Come in," she said. "My parents are going out soon."

"No," he said. "Not here. Get your things. We'll go to the pub."

She did not know what to make of him. It was impossible to tell what he was thinking. He seemed angry, restless, embarrassed.

They had walked down the street, scattering the dead blossom with their feet, not speaking. There was a pub on the corner of the next street and they stopped there. The inside had been ripped out to make one huge bar and there was jukebox music and flashing one-armed bandits. At the door Imogen hesitated. Usually he hated places like this. She expected him to walk out and find somewhere else, but he went straight to the bar and bought drinks for them both without even asking what she wanted. He led her to a corner.

"What have you been saying to Dorothea?" he said.

"Nothing," she said. "The truth. That you care about her more than you care about me."

She realised at once how childish that sounded, but it was too late.

"You're mad," he said, but he was starting to blush. The colour spread from his cheeks to his neck and even to his hands. He drank the beer very quickly, tipping back his head to pour it down his throat. "She's almost old enough to be my mother."

"What has that got to do with anything?" she said impatiently.

"You shouldn't have spoken to her," he cried. "It's upset her. She doesn't trust me anymore. She thinks I should leave the vicarage."

There was a pause and the fruit machine beside them clattered and spewed out brass tokens into a dirty metal tray. The skeletal young man who was playing the machine left them where they were and impassively pulled the handle again.

Patrick turned to her and took her hand. "You've got it all wrong," he said, trying to convince himself as much as her. "It's you I care about. You know that."

She saw then that he was ashamed of his passion for Dorothea. It scared him, made him different from all his friends. He would prefer to love her.

"Well then," she had said, standing up, wanting to get

154

her own back for all the times he had hurt her. "Why don't you prove it?"

And she had walked out of the pub, leaving him there, embarrassed and defensive. She had not seen him since then. She had waited all day at work for him to call, but there had only been the policeman with his photograph of Dorothea and the news that she was dead.

The memory of the conversation in the pub made Imogen's head spin more than measles had done when she was a girl. She got off her bed and walked to the window. She had a view of tennis courts and the bowling green and beyond to the river.

Usually there were spry old gentlemen in smart blazers bending over the green, but today it was quiet. The police must still be keeping people out of the park. At one time she had imagined herself and Patrick, old still together, but now that seemed impossible.

As she turned back from the window the phone began to ring.

When her parents came in an hour later, with arms full of exercise books, *desperate* for a gin after a day at school, the house was empty and Imogen had disappeared.

15

A_s he walked from the police station to the vicarage Ramsay tried to pinpoint what made this case so different from all his other investigations. There was the character of the victim, of course. Vicars' wives did not usually get themselves murdered. But there was, too, the point that she was emotionally involved with a quite disparate group of people, who had nothing in common but the fact that they had been caught up in Dorothea's enthusiasm or compassion. Besides her immediate family, there was Theresa Stringer with her pathetic dreams of starting a new life with Joss, the old lady with cancer in Armstrong House, and Walter Tanner, incongruously a gambler and churchwarden. In most domestic murders the suspects came from the same social group, and the rivalry and tensions which resulted in the involvement of the police arose from the situation they shared. Here, the only thing that gave the case any cohesion was Dorothea Cassidy herself.

When Ramsay arrived at the vicarage, Patrick Cassidy had still not returned and the vicar himself opened the door. The church clock was striking five-thirty and there was the same noise of commuter traffic as when the inspector had come in the morning. It was still very hot. Cassidy was flushed and anxious and a faint smell of alcohol hung about him. He seemed perpetually on the verge of hysteria. He stood in the shadowy hall and peered out at Ramsay.

"Oh dear," he said. "It's you. I had expected it to be Patrick. He drove off in my car earlier this afternoon and nobody knows where he's got to. He's a deep boy, you know. Very deep. It's impossible to tell what he's thinking even when one suspects he's in terrible pain."

Ramsay immediately noticed the change in him. Even his appearance was different. He was untidy, stooped. There was a stain on his shirt which might have been mayonnaise.

"Come in!" he said, with some desperation. He was obviously afraid of being left alone. He led Ramsay into his study, then stood, looking aimlessly round the room. The photographs he had shown Ramsay so proudly earlier in the day had been removed from the album and were scattered over the desk. One caught Ramsay's eye and he remembered where he had heard the name of the staff nurse Hunter had spoken to on the cancer ward. He said nothing and saved it for later.

"I'm so worried, you see," Cassidy said. "I can't stand it if there was another tragedy."

The words seemed prophetic and Ramsay wondered if he must know something about the death of Clive Stringer, then saw that the vicar was preoccupied with his own family, his own security. Cassidy looked up at the policeman and said simply, "I don't think I could bear to be all alone. Not now."

Then he sat heavily on the chair by the desk and stared in the garden.

"I'm afraid," Ramsay said, "I've more bad news."

The clergyman turned his head slowly to face him. He was very frightened.

"Why?" he said. "What's happened?"

Ramsay answered the unspoken question first. "It's nothing to do with Patrick," he said. "Clive Stringer died this afternoon. I understand he was one of your parishioners."

157

Cassidy leaned back in his chair.

"How dreadful!" he breathed. "Poor Clive." But Ramsay was disturbed to find in the words a sense of relief and almost of satisfaction. Cassidy showed no curiosity about how Clive had died.

"He was murdered," Ramsay said. "Almost certainly by the same person as your wife."

"Murdered?" He spoke the word slowly, as if the news was too much for him to take in. "I don't understand. . . ." Ramsay was afraid he would break down. With an effort he pulled himself together and continued. "How can I help you?"

"I have to know," Ramsay said, "what connection there could be between Clive Stringer and your wife."

"Connection?" The man repeated the word automatically. "I don't think there was any connection. Not in that sense. Dorothea brought him to church. She befriended him and his family. She was good with children. . . ."

"Was Clive made welcome in the church?" Ramsay asked. He tried to remember his last visit to an Anglican church. It was to a family baptism and the regular members of the congregation had seemed affronted by the invasion of strangers who stole their place in the pews and sang the hymns with unseemly gusto. The church had not seemed a particularly democratic organisation, and it was hard to imagine Clive Stringer mixing on equal terms with either the Walkers or Walter Tanner.

"I don't know what you mean, Inspector," Cassidy said sharply, sensing the implication behind the words. "Everyone is made welcome. The Church of England isn't a social club for the middle classes."

But as he spoke them the words seemed trite and meaningless.

"All the same," the inspector said gently, "Clive can't have been an easy person to accommodate. His language, his appearance, his delinquency must have made him an object of attention."

"Oh," Cassidy said, suddenly irritable, a bad-tempered old woman. "It was hard to ignore him. At times he was awfully disruptive. He seemed to find it impossible to sit still and would wander around the church during the service. Really, we had less trouble with the toddlers."

"Did that cause problems?"

"Not for me!" Cassidy said grandly. "But there were complaints from other members of the congregation who found it hard to concentrate on the worship. I was sympathetic but in a difficult position. I couldn't tie the boy down and there was little else I could do."

"Was there ever any question of excluding Clive Stringer from the service?" Ramsay asked.

"It was suggested to Dorothea that Clive might like to go into the hall with the Sunday-school children. To help, of course."

"Who suggested that?"

"One of our churchwardens, Walter Tanner. He's something of a traditionalist. I don't altogether share his views, but I could see that he felt very strongly about this."

"And what was your wife's reaction to the idea?"

"She dismissed it out of hand," Cassidy said unhappily. "It provided rather an argument at the parochial church council meeting. Walter Tanner threatened to resign."

Dorothea would have been magnificent, Ramsay thought. He wished he could have seen her.

"And the rest of the congregation?" he asked. "Who did they support?"

"I should say that support was fairly equally divided," Cassidy said. "Dorothea had a lot of admirers. . . . She introduced a lot of new people to the church. Young people. Families. They supported her."

"And you?" Ramsay said. "What did you think?"

159

There was a shocked silence, and for a moment Ramsay was made to feel that the direct question was an impossible breach of manners.

Then he answered bitterly: "I didn't think anything," he said. "I just wanted to stop the unpleasantness and bring people together. Besides, my opinion didn't seem to count."

He lapsed into silence again, then with something of the old charm he turned to Ramsay and smiled.

"I'm sorry, Inspector. That wasn't fair. I suppose I'm saying that I saw my role as a conciliator. Besides, I never had Dorothea's courage. . . ."

Ramsay sat forward in his chair. "I'd be grateful," he said smoothly, "if you could tell me something about Mr. Tanner. I'd like your personal opinion of his standing in the town. Was he well thought of, for example? Were there any rumours concerning his private life?"

"Of course Walter's well thought of," Cassidy said. "He's been churchwarden for years. He's highly respected. You mustn't take Dorothea's opposition to him too seriously. She was young, impatient. And the worst she said of him was that he was stuffy."

"We found your wife's car in Walter Tanner's drive this morning," Ramsay said. "And Clive Stringer's body in his house this afternoon."

"Have you arrested him?" Cassidy demanded. "Do you think he murdered Dorothea?"

Ramsay shook his head. "I don't know," he said, honestly. "I haven't reached any conclusions yet. But you can understand my interest in Mr. Tanner's relationship with your wife and Clive Stringer."

Cassidy seemed not to have taken it in. He shook his head in wonder.

"When was this acrimonious committee meeting?" Ramsay asked.

"Friday," Cassidy said. "Last Friday. A week ago."

"Would you say that Mr. Tanner had taken an active dislike to Clive Stringer?"

"I suppose I would. He talked about principles, but there did seem to be a degree of personal animosity in his reaction to the boy. Dorothea seemed to think it was a matter of ignorance—Walter had never met anyone like Clive before, she said, and was frightened by him. She thought if they got to know each other, the problem would go away. She asked them both here for tea on Sunday afternoon. I couldn't see the thing working, but she was excited at the idea. She wasn't a great one at domestic matters, but she spent all Saturday getting ready, making cakes, you know. Patrick and I had to promise to be on our best behaviour."

"Did they come?"

"Clive did. Walter, rather rudely, phoned up at the last moment to say that he had another appointment. Clive had made a real effort—I'd never seen him so smart and I think he was very upset. He sat for an hour in the kitchen thinking Tanner might change his mind. Dorothea, of course, was furious."

"Was there any reason for Clive Stringer to be in Mr. Tanner's house this afternoon?"

"No. None at all. Apart from his antipathy to the boy, Walter was a private man. He didn't invite many people to his home."

"I had understood Dorothea was a regular visitor."

"Oh yes," Cassidy said, with a sad smile. "Dorothea often went to see Walter. She had great faith in her powers of persuasion. She was convinced that eventually she would get him to agree with her ideas. But she was never invited."

Ramsay paused. He wanted to ask Cassidy about Tanner's gambling but was afraid that he might refuse to answer direct personal questions about one of his congregation. One of his men had been to the bookmaker's on the Ridgeway. They knew that Tanner had gambled heavily and lost a substantial

161

sum of money over several years. Ramsay did not know how well the man had managed to keep the habit hidden.

"Is it possible Mrs. Cassidy wanted to see Mr. Tanner about something quite different?" Ramsay asked. "If she thought he had a problem, she would offer, wouldn't she, to help?"

"I suppose so. Yes," Cassidy said. Then, genuinely curious: "But what problem could Walter have?"

Ramsay hesitated again, but this was a murder investigation and he needed information quickly.

"He bets," he said. "Very heavily. He's lost at least five thousand pounds since it all began four years ago."

"Yes," Cassidy said. "I see. That would explain a lot."

"You never suspected that he had a problem?"

"I knew that he was lonely and isolated. I hadn't realised he had turned to gambling. The poor man must have been under a terrible strain. It reflects very badly on the whole congregation. We should have done more to help."

"Did Mrs. Cassidy know, do you think?"

"I'm not sure," Cassidy said. "Perhaps."

"But she never discussed the matter with you?"

"Oh," he said. "She wouldn't do that. Not without asking Walter first. She had a great concern about confidentiality."

He spoke with pride and Ramsay thought suddenly that he had lost sight of the great affection Cassidy had felt for his wife. She had caused him inconvenience and embarrassment, but the passion which had made him run away and marry her, as if they were eloping teenagers, had remained to the end. It occurred to Ramsay that if he forgot the power of that central relationship, he would lose the focus of the whole investigation.

"If Mrs. Cassidy had discovered that Mr. Tanner was gambling regularly, what would she have done?" Ramsay asked.

"She would have talked to him," Cassidy said with certainty. "She would have gone to him and offered support, help."

And Tanner would have hated that, Ramsay thought. Nothing could be worse than being confronted by the young woman, so flawless and innocent, reminding him by comparison of his own weakness.

Cassidy got up suddenly and walked to the window, imagining for an instant the sound of a car on the drive, but he was disappointed and turned back to the room.

"I wish Patrick would come," he said. "I don't know where he could be."

"Perhaps he's with his girlfriend," Ramsay said. "You showed me a photograph earlier. Did you say her name was Imogen?"

"I don't think he's with Imogen," the vicar said. "She was here earlier looking for him."

"Is she at the university, too?" Ramsay asked.

"No, no," Cassidy said impatiently. "She's a nurse in the general hospital."

"How did Imogen and Mrs. Cassidy get on?" Ramsay asked.

"I don't know. Well enough. Patrick didn't bring her here very often. You know what young people are like."

"Would Mrs. Cassidy have had any urgent reason to speak to her yesterday?"

"No. Of course not. What is this all about?"

But Ramsay only shook his head, as if he were making polite conversation to pass the time until Patrick returned.

"Have you had any other visitors today?" he asked. "Since the Walkers brought you back to the vicarage?"

Cassidy shook his head.

"And you've been here all the time?"

"Of course," The clergyman was almost shouting. "I've been waiting for Patrick."

There was a pause and the church clock struck six.

"I'm afraid I must ask you some more questions about your movements yesterday," Ramsay said gently. "Just to confirm your story. There's been a minor discrepancy. Probably nothing important."

Cassidy stared at him blankly.

"You say that you left here at about quarter past five," Ramsay said. "Patrick said that he arrived home soon after. He just missed you, he said. We have a witness who says she saw Mrs. Cassidy's car in the drive at half-past five. She saw Patrick and Mrs. Cassidy having tea together in the kitchen. They were rather strained, she thought. Patrick never told us about that meeting. Can you think of any reason for his wanting to keep it a secret?"

"No," Cassidy said. "How should I know? You'll have to ask him."

"We will ask him," Ramsay murmured. The sun was lower than it had been in the morning and shone directly through the window, making the room breathlessly hot. Ramsay was thinking that he should leave. He imagined Hunter at Tanner's house, fuming, waiting for more instructions, for some idea of what was going on. He could send somebody else to the house to wait with Cassidy for Patrick's return. But just as he was about to go, the vicar, oppressed, it seemed, by the heat and the silence and the tension of waiting for his son, began to talk.

"I think Dorothea must have been disappointed in me," he said. "Before we married she only knew me really, from my books, and they were written a long time ago. It is rather easy to stand up for one's principles in print. I think she must have been disappointed in the coward she had married."

"And Dorothea?" Ramsay asked. "Did she have principles?"

The vicar sat forward in his chair. "I rather think," he said, "that she had too many."

Then he settled back, apparently lost in thought, and when Ramsay said he would have to go, he made no effort to keep him there.

16

W*alter Tanner* sat in the dusty living room and stared with increasing hostility at Gordon Hunter. Although the policeman had arrived more than an hour before, he had only just begun to give Tanner his full attention. At the start it had been noise and self-important bustle, with Hunter standing in the hall directing a stream of strangers upstairs. There were still police cars outside and a small crowd of the less inhibited neighbours gathered to watch. From the landing came loud men's voices and someone was whistling. For a moment Tanner felt something of the excitement and exhilaration that came to him when he was gambling. In the betting shop there was noise, a breathless sense of risk, and the feeling that in the minutes of watching the horses on the television in the corner of the shop, he was really living. This is a gamble, he thought, as somebody else came to open the door and stamped up the stairs without waiting for an invitation. How much I tell the police, how I play the situation, it's all a gamble. Then he looked at Hunter's face and thought that, as in the bookmaker's, the punter was always destined to lose.

"You can't expect me to believe that this is all coincidence," Hunter said. He was standing, leaning against a solid bookcase with one shoulder. He thought that this was

166

his big chance for promotion and he was convinced Tanner was a murderer. I'll show Ramsay that you don't have to have been to the grammar to get results! he thought. "A murdered woman's car and now the boy's body," he said. "It's about time you started telling us what it's all about. Where were you this afternoon?"

Tanner took a deep breath. This was it. He was under starter's orders.

"I was on the Ridgeway Estate," he said.

"Were you visiting someone," Hunter demanded. "Was it Stringer? Something to do with the church?"

Tanner smiled and showed uneven nicotine-stained teeth. Keep it light, he thought. Keep it confident. Make it seem that there's nothing to hide. Some of it they'll find out anyway.

"No, Sergeant," Tanner said. "Hardly that. I was there to visit my bookmaker."

"Do you expect me to believe that?" Hunter said. "Are you trying to be funny?"

"Not at all, Sergeant. I have a little flutter occasionally. Nothing substantial, of course. It's a little harmless fun since I retired."

"There *were* witnesses," Hunter said.

"Of course, Sergeant. Of course."

And they had not got much further than that when Ramsay arrived from the vicarage. He had been back to the station to pick up a car, and Hunter watched it draw up with anger and disappointment.

That was typical, he thought. Ramsay had arrived to steal the glory, just as Tanner was about to confess. But Ramsay, it seemed, was unconvinced about Tanner's guilt. Hunter met him in the hall and tried to persuade him to take the retired grocer to the police station for questioning.

"Put him in the cells for an hour," he said. "That'll persuade him to talk."

"How does he seem?" Ramsay asked.

"Cocky. Too bloody cocky. Seems to find it funny."

"Perhaps he's hysterical," Ramsay said. There was, after all, something ridiculous about a body in a bath. It was like a second-rate horror movie.

"But the evidence!" Hunter said. "The car and the boy's body. And now you tell me there was motive, too. The vicar's wife had found out about his gambling and Tanner couldn't stand the lad. It's too much of a coincidence."

"Perhaps the murderer has a perverse sense of humor," Ramsay said. "Or a grudge against the old man. And we don't know that Dorothea had found out about the gambling. It's a possibility."

He was distant, as if his attention was elsewhere and he was going through the motions of considering Hunter's opinion. Of all the inspector's moods Hunter found this the most irritating.

"Is there anything else I should know?" he demanded. "Something relevant which might be worth a mention?"

Ramsay blinked as if shocked by the crude sarcasm, but he answered calmly.

"Dorothea Cassidy went back to the vicarage late yesterday afternoon. She met Patrick. The witness says the atmosphere was strained, but she's deaf, so she's probably rather unreliable. And I know who Dorothea went to see in the hospital yesterday."

Hunter remained defiantly silent. He would not give Ramsay the satisfaction of asking for the information.

"It was the staff nurse you spoke to," Ramsay said. "Her name's Buchan. Imogen Buchan. She's Patrick Cassidy's girlfriend."

Hunter swore under his breath.

"There is something else," Ramsay said. There bloody would be, Hunter thought. "Joss Corkhill saw Dorothea Cassidy at the fair last night. Or he says he did. He might be a malicious witness playing games, but I think I believe him. She was with a young woman whose description fits that of Imogen Buchan. Joss should be at the fair all night. We'll send someone round with a photo to make sure.''

Still, Hunter insisted that they should take Walter Tanner to the police station, but Ramsay refused. The double murder had attracted the attention of the national press. They were jumpy and took delight in coming too quickly to conclusions. The phrase ''helping the police with their enquiries'' would be seen by them as a euphemism. Annie Ramsay's evidence made it impossible that Walter had killed Clive. Even if the boy were waiting for Tanner inside the house, he would hardly have had time to commit the murder between arriving home and phoning the police. There was Dorothea, of course. There was still a chance that Tanner had killed her. But in that case who had murdered Clive? And what could be the motive? Ramsay felt that Tanner was useful because he had been close to Dorothea and understood the politics of the church rather than as a suspect in his own right.

When Ramsay returned to the room, Tanner was standing up, smoking a cigarette. He looked at Ramsay hopefully, seeing him as an ally, someone to rescue him from the bullying Hunter. Ramsay took a seat, waited until Tanner had stubbed out the cigarette, then spoke quietly.

''When did Mrs. Cassidy find out about your gambling?'' he asked.

Walter stared at him, his mouth slightly open. He clearly thought the man must be some sort of magician. He was too shocked to deny it.

''Well,'' Ramsay persisted gently. ''It was a recent discovery, wasn't it?''

This was a guess, but he imagined that Dorothea would never allow a situation she considered unsatisfactory to go on indefinitely. She would use all her energy to do something about it.

169

Walter Tanner nodded.

"How did she find out?"

"She'd been visiting a family on the Ridgeway," Walter said unhappily. "She saw me going into the bookie's." The exhilaration which had sustained him through the interview with Hunter had left him.

"What did she do?" Ramsay asked.

Tanner paused, trying to find the words, stammering over them, and when he spoke, Ramsay was surprised by the power of them.

"She tormented me," he said. "She was so certain . . . so morally superior . . . so horribly kind." And so beautiful, he thought. A vicar's wife had no right to be so beautiful.

"What did she expect you to do?"

"To stop, of course," Tanner said. "She seemed to think that it would be easy. 'I really don't see the problem,' she said. 'You don't need that sort of thing. Not you, Walter. Not with your faith.' "

"But it wasn't that easy?"

"It was impossible," he said. "I knew she was right and I tried to give it up, but it was like a terrible addiction." He paused again and ran his tongue over his lips. "Then she thought I should make the whole thing public. She said I needed the support and encouragement of the whole congregation. If it remained a secret, I'd never stop."

"Did she threaten to tell the others?" Ramsay asked.

"No," Walter said. "To be fair, she never did that. But she was always here, putting pressure on me. 'Why don't you tell them at the PCC meeting?' she would say, and then throughout the meeting she would be there, staring at me, waiting for me to speak. She didn't see that her interference just made things worse. It made me realise what a mess I'd made of my life. I couldn't stand it."

"When was Mrs. Cassidy last here?" Ramsay asked.

"On Saturday morning," he said. "She came to ask me to Sunday afternoon tea."

"But you didn't go," Ramsay said. "Did you?"

"No," he said. "I couldn't face it."

"Did you kill her?"

"No," he said with a strange, comic dignity. "I wouldn't have killed her."

There was a pause, the sound of footsteps on the stairs, the slam of the front door. The house was suddenly quiet.

"Has anyone else got a key to your house?" Ramsay asked. "The lock wasn't forced."

Then after some thought: "No," Walter said. "When my mother was ill, a woman came in to look after her. She had a spare key. I don't think we ever got it back."

"How do you explain the fact that the door was open?"

"I don't know. I suppose I forgot to lock it when I went out. I was upset."

"Tell me about Clive Stringer," Ramsay said. "Why did you dislike him so much?"

"I didn't dislike him," Walter said. "Not really. It was what he represented."

"What was that?"

"I suppose," Walter said slowly, "he represented all the changes Dorothea had made in the church. He made me uncomfortable."

"You have no idea what he was doing here this afternoon?"

"None," Tanner said. "If Dorothea had been alive, I would have suspected her of sending him here. She had some silly idea that we might be friends. But of course that's impossible."

"Yes," Ramsay said. "That's impossible." He felt a sudden deep sympathy for this sad little man. The violation of his privacy by the murderer was a crime in itself.

From outside, a long way off and distorted by amplification, came the sound of rock music. The carnival parade was about to start. Ramsay realised it was already evening. On the Ridgeway Estate Hilary Masters was waiting with Theresa Stringer to speak to him. It was too hot, too complicated, and he longed for a moment to escape to his cottage in Heppleburn, where there would be a breeze up the valley from the sea and complete silence. He stood up.

"Are you going?" Walter Tanner said in a panic. Perhaps he was afraid that he would be left again to Gordon Hunter.

"Yes," Ramsay said. "We'll both go now and leave you in peace. Someone will be back later to take a statement."

On the doorstep he paused. Hunter was waiting by the front gate, angry that his opinion had been disregarded, fuming. Ramsay wanted to say something to Tanner to show him that he thought well of him. What right had Dorothea to judge him so harshly? He knew what it was like to be lonely, unpopular, frustrated.

"Mrs. Cassidy must have cared about you," he said, "to have shown so much interest."

But the thought seemed to give Tanner no consolation. "She cared too much about everyone," he said. "That was the problem."

He stood in the porch and watched the men walk down the street toward their cars.

Beside the cars the men paused. Ramsay could sense Hunter's hostility but had neither the patience nor the skill to deal with it. Perhaps the tension, the edge of competition made them more effective, he thought, but life would have been more comfortable if they could have got on.

"What do you want me to do now?" Hunter asked.

"Go back to the station and coordinate the team working the fair," Ramsay said. "We'll need photos of Dorothea and Imogen. That was the last time Dorothea was seen. You could see if you can get hold of the Buchan girl, too. If she was working this morning, she should be free now. The hospital will have an address and phone number for her. She might know where Patrick Cassidy is."

Hunter nodded reluctantly. It made sense.

"I'm going to the Ridgeway," Ramsay said, "to talk to the boy's mother. Miss Masters from the social services is with her."

He added the last sentence as an afterthought, dropping it in as if it had no significance, but Hunter was not fooled. He smirked, imagining the interest he could stir up in the canteen. Ramsay and the Snow Queen, he would say, his voice full of innuendo. They'd make a good team. The thought cheered him up and he drove away.

It took Hunter longer than he had expected to find out where Imogen lived. There was no Buchan in the phone book. Her parents, fearing malicious calls about kids at school, were ex-directory. When he phoned the vicarage, thinking that someone there would surely know where to find her, the vicar was vague and unhelpful. Patrick had still not come home, he said. He feared another dreadful tragedy. Hunter listened to his ravings for a while then replaced the receiver while he was still in midstream. The hospital was suspicious. By now all the administrative staff had gone home and the ward sister was unwilling to take the responsibility of passing on personal information over the phone. He persuaded her in the end by allowing her to call him back, after she had checked his number. When at last he had the information he needed, he dialled the number, but there was no reply.

Almost immediately afterwards he was told that a Mr. and Mrs. Buchan were at the front desk. They wanted to report their daughter missing. Hunter saw the Buchans in a small interview room. It had no natural light. Hunter had been eating fish and chips and the smell of it clung to his clothes. The Buchans were embarrassed and apologetic. Of course, Imogen was a grown woman, they said. They realised she had her own life to lead. They would be the last people to

173

question her right to independence. It was this business with Dorothea Cassidy which worried them. Dorothea had been so close to them, a great friend. It was only natural, wasn't it, that they should be worried.

Hunter tried to contain his excitement. There was probably nothing sinister in Imogen's disappearance. These were middle-class parents whose daughter had fancied a bit of life without telling them.

"Has she got a boyfriend?" he asked in his specially perfected bored voice, though he knew the answer already. The last thing he wanted was for them to panic.

"Of course," Mrs. Buchan said. "I thought we'd explained. She's going out with Patrick Cassidy. That's why we're so concerned."

"And she's not with him now?"

"Apparently not. He seems to have disappeared, too."

Surely that was significant, Hunter thought. Patrick Cassidy had lied about meeting his stepmother the afternoon before. Dorothea had rushed to Newcastle to speak to Imogen at work and had probably been seen with her at the fair during the evening. Now the pair of them had vanished. It was all down to him now, he thought. Ramsay had left him in charge while he went off to play social workers with Theresa Stringer on the Ridgeway Estate. He had the opportunity of reaching a conclusion to this case on his own.

Mrs. Buchan was still talking. "She seems to have been under such a strain lately," she said. "It's not easy, of course, working with the terminally ill and she has such dedication. . . ."

"When was she last seen?" Hunter asked.

"She finished her shift at two o'clock," Mrs. Buchan said. Her husband seemed lost in thoughts of his own and content to let her do all the talking. "She came straight back to Otterbridge and went to the vicarage to see if Patrick was there. He wasn't. She must have come home then, because her car's parked outside. I expected her to be there when we came in from work, but there was no sign of her. I wasn't worried at first, of course. I thought she'd gone into town to do some shopping. Otterbridge is such fun during festival time, isn't it? But now the shops have been closed for hours. She hasn't many friends, you know, besides Patrick, and I can't think where she might be.''

"Perhaps she's at the fair," he said. "Does she enjoy going?"

They were noncommittal, as if they had no real idea what she did enjoy.

"Did she go out yesterday evening?"

She went out with Patrick, they said. She hadn't told them where they were going.

"What time did she come back?"

Mrs. Buchan shrugged. "I don't know," she said. "We were back rather late ourselves. It was the festival ball." She paused and looked at him as if he were one of her remedial fourth-formers. "She didn't disappear last night, you know. I saw her at home this morning, before she went to work.''

He was apologetic, understanding. He realised that, he said. It was a question of finding a pattern, of working out where she might be. There was probably nothing to worry about. The carnival seemed to have gone to everyone's heads. She would be out, watching the procession with the rest of the town. He would circulate the photo they had brought, make a few enquiries. They were to leave it to him.

The Buchans left the police station reassured, charmed by him.

17

It took Ramsay longer than he had expected to get to the Ridgeway. His drive across town coincided with the start of the parade, and none of the roads he tried were clear. Front Street was closed to traffic, cordoned off with plastic bunting which reminded him of the tape they had used to mark the area where Dorothea's body had been found. As he sat in a queue of cars he heard the rhythmic crash of the brass band which always led the procession. It conflicted with the fairground music and the amplified noise from some of the floats. He could see nothing from the car, but he could picture the event. As a child he had always been brought to Otterbridge for the carnival and nothing had changed very much. Behind the band would be a group of miners, carrying the banner of a pit which had closed years before but which was still given pride of place. His father had worked down the pits but had refused to take part in the parade.

"Look at them," he would say. "Dressed up like a cartload of monkeys. So much for the dignity of the workingman."

There would be children in fancy dress, and the sworddance team, and the lorries carrying floats, elaborate tableaux celebrating local charities and businesses. When he

176

was a child, the floats had fascinated him. What it must be like, he had thought, to ride up there above the crowd, waving! But when, one year, Annie had arranged for him to dress up and be on the church float with her, he had refused, horrified at the suggestion. The line of traffic started to move slowly and he drove on.

He had never seen the town so busy. Perhaps the heat of the evening made it impossible for people to stay indoors. They jostled in a stream along the pavement, spilling occasionally into the street, so Ramsay was forced to stop again.

There were family parties, the children made nervous and fretful by the crowd, groups of teenage boys, high-spirited and loud, clutching cans of lager, and groups of young women, giggling in fancy dress. The pubs were all full and customers were forced onto the pavements with their drinks. It was an explosive mix, Ramsay thought: the hot evening, the alcohol, the gangs of young men all set on showing off. He was glad he did not have the responsibility of policing it. As he was forced to stop again to allow a pack of cub scouts to cross the road in an orderly crocodile, he thought he saw Joss Corkhill, coming out of an off-licence with a bottle in his hand, but when the traffic moved again, he had disappeared.

At last he was clear of the town and he drove quickly along the bypass toward the Ridgeway, knowing that he was a fool to hurry because Hilary Masters would have given up waiting by now. But when he got to Hardy Street, her car was still there, parked outside the house, and through the window he could see the two women sitting together on the sofa. Hilary Masters was turned toward him, and when she saw him she smiled. It was a smile of welcome and relief, and suddenly he was a young man again, plucking up the courage to ask some girl to go out with him, thinking: Perhaps with this one I've a chance of pulling it off. Perhaps this one fancies me.

Hilary Masters stood up and came into the hall to open the door to him.

"I'm sorry I'm so late," he said. "I hope I haven't caused you any inconvenience."

He could hear the words as they were spoken, as distant and formal as Hilary had been on their first meeting. He wished he could start again.

"That's all right," she said. She smiled again and looked very tired. "Really. I would have waited anyway. I don't think Theresa's in any state to be left alone. The doctor gave her something to calm her, but it seems just to have made her confused. I'm not sure you'll get any sense out of her tonight." She stood close to him and spoke softly, looking through the door toward Theresa.

"Did she tell you anything?" he asked.

She shook her head. "Not very much. Clive left the house before we did this afternoon. She didn't see him again. She thought he was going to work." She paused. "Where's Joss?" she asked. "Theresa will want to know. She's been asking for him."

"We let him go," he said. "He couldn't have killed Clive and I don't think he met Dorothea yesterday afternoon."

She seemed worried by the news and he wondered if she had some inside knowledge. Perhaps Theresa had confided in her and she felt unable to pass on the information.

"He hasn't been here," she said.

"I don't think he will come back," he said. "He was talking about leaving."

"Poor Theresa," she said. "It was bound to happen sometime, but he might have waited."

She turned back to the room where Theresa sat, quite still, and waited for him to follow her.

The room was stiflingly hot and airless. He looked at the poster of mountains and sea and thought that if he were Joss Corkhill, he would run away, too. Unable to breathe, he opened a window. The estate was silent, empty. Usually at this time on a sunny evening it would have been at its most lively with children on bikes, adults on their way out, but even the ice-cream vans had deserted the place for the centre of town. The Ridgeway Community Association was entering its first float, and though no one thought it had a chance of winning, they all wanted to be there to cheer it on. He turned back to the room.

Theresa Stringer stared at him, bewildered. He was not even sure if she remembered who he was.

"I'm sorry about Clive," he said.

She shook her head as if she were unable to take it in.

"You took Joss away," she said. "What have you done with him?"

Would it be kinder, Ramsay thought, to lie, to tell her that Joss was still in custody? He could not do it.

"We let him go," Ramsay said. "We haven't charged him."

"Oh," she said, and he thought she was relieved, though it was hard to tell. "I expect he's at the fair then. Or the pub. He'll be back later, when they throw him out."

And she gave a little smile, as if that had been an attempt at a joke.

"Yes," Ramsay said. "Perhaps," He looked at Hilary Masters, hoping that she might explain that Corkhill was unlikely to return, but she seemed preoccupied and he thought again she might be keeping something from him. He was afraid of being, in her eyes, the heavy-handed policeman and he did not pry.

"Where's my baby?" Theresa cried suddenly, like a child waking up in the middle of a nightmare. "I want my baby."

Hilary Masters sat beside her again on the sofa and took her hand.

"Ssh," she said. "Ssh. Beverley's quite safe. You know

179

that. She's with her foster mother. I'll take you to see her tomorrow.''

Her voice was low, caressing. Ramsay was very moved.

"No!" Theresa said. "No!" But the outburst passed and quite suddenly she returned to her state of blank incomprehension.

"Tell me about Clive," Ramsay said gently. "Do you know who killed him?''

She stared at him, obviously terrified. "I don't know anything,'' she whispered. "You ask Joss. He'll tell you how I don't know anything.''

"Do you think Joss killed Clive?'' he asked. Her reaction surprised him. He had expected grief, confusion, but not this fear.

"I don't know anything,'' she repeated, clinging to Hilary's arm for support.

"It's no good," Hilary said. "I really don't think she can help you.'' The women stared at him together, so he felt cruel, heartless in persisting.

"I'd like to see Clive's bedroom,'' he said, knowing he was only putting off the unpleasant task until later. He knew he would have to talk to Theresa that night. However confused she was, there were still questions which had to be answered. Surely Hilary would understand that. He hoped he might find in Clive's room something which would provide a focus for the questions, something to start them off. Besides, it would give him a break from this stuffy room and the accusing eyes of the women.

Hilary turned to Theresa. "Is that all right?'' she said. "You don't mind?"

Theresa shook her head and he left the room and climbed the stairs. Clive's bedroom was small, square, and surprisingly tidy. It was at the back of the house. The bed was made and the faded greyish sheet was folded back over a threadbare blanket made of different-coloured knitted squares. Built into

180

an alcove there was a wardrobe which obviously came as a standard fitting to the council house, and there was a kitchen chair beside the bed, but there was no other furniture. Ramsay opened the wardrobe door. Most of the clothes were piled on shelves at the bottom. He took the garments out one at a time. Occasionally he came across something new which had obviously been a present from Dorothea—there was a brown T-shirt with an Oxfam logo and a bright hand-knitted sweater—but the rest had the limp shapeless look of old jumble.

Inside the wardrobe door was stuck a photograph of Dorothea and Clive together, standing formally outside the vicarage. Clive upright and proud and grinning broadly. Was it tact, Ramsay wondered, which had caused him to hide the photo away? Did he think his mother would be hurt by his affection for the vicar's wife?

Ramsay looked under the bed and found a pile of comics and a lot of dust. On the chair by the bed was a plastic mug of water and Clive's watch. That, too, Ramsay remembered, had been a present from Dorothea. Clive had been wearing it the day before when he waited for her to come out of Mrs. Bowman's flat in Armstrong House. I never asked the old lady about that, he thought. I never followed up the discrepancies in their stories. He could not see why it would be important, but the thought of the watch troubled him, niggled throughout the rest of his conversation with Theresa. Before going downstairs, he paused and looked out of the boy's window and wished again that he could be in Heppleburn.

In the living room it seemed that the women had hardly moved. He found that he had no patience with either of them.

"Coffee!" he said briskly. "I think we could all do with some coffee. Perhaps you could make some for us, Miss Masters."

The social worker looked surprised, but she went into the kitchen. Theresa watched her go with terror.

"Theresa," he said. He tried to sound kind but realised that the effect was patronizing. Fatherly concern did not suit him. "I came to talk to you earlier. Perhaps you remember. . . ."

She nodded.

"You didn't tell me what Dorothea talked about when she came here late yesterday afternoon," he said. "It would be helpful if we knew what her plans for the rest of the evening were. Has anything come back to you?"

She was more alert now, and very tense.

"It was nothing important," she said. "She just came to see how I was feeling."

"Tell me about Clive then," he said, keeping his voice calm. "When he left here today, where did you think he was going?"

"Back to work," she said. "You were here, weren't you? You heard what he said."

"Was it usual for him to come home for his lunch? It's a long way."

"It depended what he felt like," she said. "They weren't paying him."

"But he was there to do community service," Ramsay said. "He wouldn't have been allowed just to wander about."

Hilary Masters came in then, carrying mugs of coffee, holding them awkwardly by the handles, all in one hand.

"It wasn't really community service," she said. "Not in the legal sense. He was a juvenile. He was placed on a supervision order and the arrangement to work at the old people's home was made informally between Dorothea and the warden."

"So he never worked set hours," Ramsay asked.

"He was supposed to," she said, "but it was hard to keep him to a timetable. He was easily distracted."

182

Ramsay remembered that the same thing had been said about Dorothea. He wondered if the boy's inability to stick to anything had been a factor in his death. Had his attention been caught by something the murderer wanted kept secret? Had he, in his vacant, bumbling way, become involved in Dorothea's murder?

"He might have gone to the fair," Theresa said suddenly. "He always liked the fair."

Ramsay put the mug to his mouth but found the liquid inside almost undrinkable. Hilary had put milk in it and he wondered if she would ever know him well enough to realise that he always drank it black.

This is ludicrous, he thought. I'm so tired. I can't think straight. Outside in the street there was the sound of a car horn being hit over and over again, laughter, a car radio played far too loud. Someone had started their celebrations before reaching the town.

"Did Clive tell you anything?" he said. "Anything which might help us find out who killed him?"

Theresa shook her head and looked at him over the rim of her coffee cup, like some stupid, frightened animal.

"He never talked to me," she said sadly. "Not once Mrs. Cassidy started visiting." She paused. "I expect it was my fault, too. Things were different after Joss came to stay."

"Did he have any enemies? Anyone who disliked him enough to kill him?"

Theresa set the coffee cup on the floor at her feet.

"Only that man at the church," she said deliberately.

"You mean Walter Tanner?" Ramsay said. "The church-warden who didn't want Clive to take part in the service?"

"No," she said. "Not him. I mean the vicar, Dorothea's husband. He hated Clive."

"What do you mean?" he demanded. "How do you know?"

But by now the exchange seemed to have exhausted her.

She lay back on the sofa with her eyes closed. Perhaps the sedation given by the doctor was just starting to take effect, perhaps it was a way of avoiding more questions. Ramsay felt the urge to shake her. What right had she to escape into a drugged sleep? he thought. But he said nothing, aware that any attempt to disturb Theresa now would be interpreted by Hilary as brutality. He stood up.

"I'm sorry," Hilary said. "I told you she wouldn't be much help. It's all been too much for her to cope with."

"What will you do with her now?"

"Wait till she wakes then take her home with me. I don't think she should be left alone and I don't like the idea of staying here."

She paused. This is it, he thought. She's giving me the chance to find out where she lives. But he was nervous as a boy and he could not ask for the address. He could always find out.

"Perhaps if Theresa feels like it, we'll stop to watch the carnival," Hilary continued. "She's like a child. She'd enjoy it. It may stop her brooding for a while."

"You're very patient with her," he said.

She shrugged. "It's my job. Besides, I explained. Theresa's always been special, my first client. She trusts me. It's a responsibility."

And how can I compete with that? he thought. He saw clearly for the first time how frustrating it must have been for Diana, his ex-wife, competing for his attention against the responsibilities of his job.

They stood awkwardly on the doorstep. A mongrel ran along the pavement and cocked a leg by the wheel of his car.

"Look," she said. "When this is all over, perhaps I could cook you a meal. Show you that all social workers don't live on lentils."

"Yes," he said. "I'd like that." He realised that he was beaming.

When? he wanted to ask. When can I come? Instead he wrote his home telephone number on a scrap of paper and shyly handed it to her.

In the car he talked to Hunter on the radio and learned that Imogen Buchan had been reported missing.

"The boy hasn't gone back to the vicarage either," Hunter said. "Do you think they've done a runner?"

Ramsay was indecisive. "I don't know," he said. "I'll leave it to you. They might be at the carnival like everyone else." Yet he thought there was a desperation about the murders which might indicate the intensity of youth. "Put out a general alert," he said. "We've got to find them." Then, again: "I'll leave all the arrangements to you."

He had become preoccupied by the difference in the accounts of Dorothea's return to Armstrong House. Clive had been the only witness to suggest that Dorothea and Emily Bowman had spent a long time together and now he was dead. It might only be coincidence, but he should speak to the old lady and sort the matter out. He pulled away from the kerb, aware that Hilary Masters, standing by the window in Theresa's front room, was watching him.

 **18**

It was nine o'clock and the sun was low in the sky, orange, diffused on the edges by thin cloud. At last Emily Bowman's room was in shadow. She felt comfortable for the first time that day. She sat in the same chair by the window and tried, as she had every evening for the past two weeks, to compose a letter to leave behind after her suicide. All around her the building was quiet. Most of the other residents had gathered in the rooms overlooking the main street to watch the parade. At teatime Annie Ramsay had turned up with scones you could break a tooth on and had tried to persuade her to go, too.

"Come on, pet," she had said. "We've all had a shock, but there's no point brooding. H'away now, we'd like your company."

Would they still want my company, Emily Bowman thought, if they knew what I'd done?"

She had eaten a scone to please her visitor and then claimed fatigue. Annie had scampered away to get ready. Reggie Younger had invited her into his flat, she said. She'd always had a soft spot for Reggie and you had a good view from there. Especially from the bedroom.

Emily Bowman had been aware of the parade passing along the busy street but had taken little notice. Still the right words for her letter would not come. She wanted to justify the decision, persuade the reader, as she had been unable to persuade Dorothea, that she was doing the right thing. And, she thought, though the letter would probably be found by the warden or by Annie Ramsay, it was to Dorothea that she would be writing. She wanted to make it clear that she was not a coward. It was not the pain which frightened her. It was the inconclusive tedium. To spend the rest of one's days waiting, aimless, seemed wickedly inefficient. Her only sense in all the waiting—for the ambulance, in the hospital corridor—was that she was in the way.

She watched Ramsay park his car in Armstrong Street. She recognised him from the weekly consultations. The parade had moved on and the streets were deserted. She wondered for a moment if Annie would welcome the visit. She had planned, Emily knew, to spend all evening with Reggie Younger. When Ramsay knocked at her door, she did not ask him in, but directed him down the corridor to where he might find his aunt.

"No, no," he said. "I'd like to talk to you."

He stood in the doorway, grave, still, and she was reminded for a moment of a young priest she had known when she was a girl and who she had dreamed, for a while, of marrying. The memory of the old excitement surprised her. She had never felt that way about her husband.

"Well," she said, hiding her confusion with brusqueness. "You'd better come in."

He sat opposite her, and in the shadow she could hardly make out the expression on his face.

"Mrs. Bowman," he said. "I've come to find out why you have lied to the police."

For a moment she thought of making a fight of it, of denying everything. There was no way he could find out now what had happened between her and Dorothea. Then he looked up, so the light caught his face, and she saw that he was really interested in her, in a way that the doctors and the nurses with their professional understanding had never been. It occurred to her that if she talked to him, she would never have to write the letter.

"You did lie, Mrs. Bowman, didn't you, about the time Mrs. Cassidy left you, yesterday afternoon? She came into your room and spent at least half an hour with you. We have a witness who can confirm that."

We had a witness, he thought, and held his breath to see if she swallowed it.

"Yes, Inspector. I'm afraid that I lied." The last of the light left the room and she got up awkwardly to switch on a tall standard lamp with a heavy fringed shade which stood in one corner.

"Why did you do that?"

"Because I wanted the conversation between Dorothea and me to remain confidential."

She looked at him with something of her old defiance.

"You do see," he said gently, "that now that's impossible?"

"It doesn't seem important anymore," she said.

"Dorothea came into your flat when she brought you back from the hospital?"

"Yes," she said. "She was in a hurry, but I asked her to come. There was something I wanted to discuss with her."

"Would you tell me what that was?"

She stared at him, her hands knotted on the bony lap. She wanted to believe that he would understand.

"It was a question of morality," she said. He did not reply and waited for her to continue. Why did he have so much more patience with Emily Bowman, he wondered, than he did for Theresa Stringer?

"I was considering taking my own life," she said quickly. "I wanted her views."

She was pleased to see that she had not shocked him and

that he felt no inclination to laugh. He considered her words carefully.

"You must have known," he said, "what Mrs. Cassidy's position would be."

Emily Bowman paused. I admired her, she thought. I expected too much of her. She wanted to explain.

"I hadn't expected," she said slowly, "that she would be so . . . rigid."

Emily remembered Dorothea's horror when, stumbling, she had tried to explain her intentions, her motives: "You can't even think of it," Dorothea had said. "You know it's quite wrong."

Ramsay waited for Emily to continue. Again she was reminded of the young priest. She wanted to be honest with him.

"I had always thought her sympathetic," Emily Bowman said. "Open to new ideas. We had considered her rather progressive. Her reaction came as a shock. She spoke, even, about the devil. It wasn't very helpful."

It had been horrible, she thought. Dorothea's certainty, her energy, her impersonal pity had been demeaning. It had reduced Emily to an example in a theological argument.

"Did you kill her?" Ramsay asked.

Emily moved in her chair.

"I just wanted to stop her talking," she said. "She *would* go on about the sanctity of life. There was a bread knife on the table—she'd had no lunch and I'd made her a sandwich. I picked up the knife and turned toward her. She didn't realise. She was very trusting. She kept on talking, telling me all the things I didn't want to hear, too *good* for me to bear. You're young and you wouldn't understand. I meant to kill her. What right did she have to stand there preaching? How could she know?"

"What happened?" Ramsay asked.

189

"I missed," she said simply. "I meant to kill her and I missed. I didn't even have the strength for that."

"But you cut her wrist," he said. "Didn't you?"

"Yes," she said. "And there was, I suppose, some satisfaction in that. There was a lot of blood. And at least she was quiet for a while."

"She must have been very shocked," he said, smiling.

"No," she said. "Not very. I don't think anything shocked her. And she was too busy, I think, trying to save my soul."

"Well," he said. "She must have convinced you."

"Because I'm still alive, Inspector?" She seemed to find the idea amusing. "Perhaps you're right. Perhaps she was more persuasive than I like to admit. Or perhaps I'm less brave than I thought I was."

She sat back in the chair, preoccupied with her own thoughts. Ramsay thought she was a formidable woman. He hoped she was telling the truth now. If she were lying, it would be impossible to tell.

"What time did Mrs. Cassidy leave here?" he asked.

"At about quarter past four. Your aunt appeared almost immediately afterwards. The game of bingo in the common room had just finished—that usually ends at quarter past I think."

"Wasn't Dorothea worried about leaving you alone?"

"Not too worried," Emily said. She smiled. "She had enormous faith, you know. Besides, I promised her I wouldn't take all my pills last night. It was the only way to get rid of her."

"Did she come to see you later?"

"No," Emily said. "I was surprised. She said she would come, either before her talk to the residents' association or afterwards. When she didn't come, I thought she'd given up on me. It was quite a relief."

"Did Dorothea tell you where she intended to go after leaving here yesterday afternoon?"

190

"I'm not sure," she said. "She said so much I found it rather exhausting."

"Please," he said. "Do try to remember."

She looked up at him. "Of course," she said. "Don't misunderstand me, Inspector. Despite what I said, I liked Dorothea Cassidy and admired her conviction. I was jealous of it. I'm not deliberately trying to obstruct your investigation."

He stood up and moved towards her to look out of the window. The curtains of Walter Tanner's front room were drawn against the prying eyes of the neighbours. A uniformed policeman stood outside.

"She was going to see Clive Stringer's mother," Emily Bowman said suddenly. "We saw Clive leave the building and walk toward the bus stop over there and Dorothea said, 'Poor Clive, I don't know how he's going to react to it all.' "

"Did she explain what she meant?"

"No."

"You have heard," Ramsay said, "that Clive Stringer was killed this afternoon?"

She would not meet his eyes. "Yes," she said. "I'd heard."

"Were you here all afternoon? Did you see him?"

"No," she said. "I noticed he'd gone missing when your sergeant gave me the lift to the hospital. I should have said something then, but it was always happening. He was always wandering off."

"And later this afternoon?" he persisted. "Did you see anything then?"

She shook her head.

"I was in this chair," she said, "but I was asleep. The treatment always makes me tired."

"You knew them both," he said. "You must have some ideas. Tell me about them."

Of all the people he had talked to that day he thought she

191

saw the situation most clearly. At first she was suspicious. She thought he was flattering her, then she saw the ghost of her old lover, and she began to speak. She wanted to show him how perceptive she was, how clever.

"Dorothea was a fanatic," she said. "I didn't realise to what extent until she came here yesterday. She was ruled by her conscience, by principle. I suppose I should find that admirable, but it didn't make her easy to get on with. Principles are all very well, but you shouldn't let them get out of hand. She thought compromise was wicked."

Ramsay said nothing. Was this leading anywhere or was it Emily's response to being lectured the day before?

"She would have had more sense if she'd had a family of her own," she said. "She could never have children. She tried to accept it, but it wasn't easy for her. I was late having a family and I know what it was like—watching your friends with babies, holding them, feeling jealous every time you saw a woman in a maternity smock in the street. It affected her. If she had had children, perhaps she wouldn't have felt the need so much to look after the rest of us."

"Did she treat you all like children?"

She nodded. "She thought she knew what was best for us."

"And Clive?" he asked. "Where did he fit in?"

"He was a ready-made son," she said. "Dependent, simple as a five-year-old, desperate for affection. What more could she want? We thought she was being so kind, so generous. But it wasn't good for the lad. He already had a mother. It was a dangerous way to carry on. It confused him."

"What are you saying?" he said. "Do you know who killed them?"

She shook her head, disappointed because he could not understand that she only wanted to explain how things were.

"She had another ready-made son, too," he said. "The stepson, Patrick. Did she try to mother him, too?"

192

"She tried," Emily said, "but the last thing he wanted was mothering." Ramsay looked at her.

"She was an attractive woman," she said. "She charmed them all. She couldn't help it. She probably enjoyed it. We all like a bit of flattery."

"But Patrick Cassidy has a girlfriend," Ramsay said.

"That makes no difference." She spoke sharply because he was questioning her judgement. "I saw the way he looked at her. The vicar saw it, too, but his head's so deep in the sand he wouldn't do anything about it. It wasn't healthy the three of them living there."

Ramsay remembered the brooding, unhappy poems in Patrick's room and thought they must have been written for Dorothea, not Imogen.

"I see," he said. And he felt he knew Dorothea Cassidy for the first time. She had charmed him, too.

They sat in silence. Outside, it was almost dark. He stared blankly out of the window and he saw the case, too, as if he had come to it freshly, with a new perspective. He thought of Joss Corkhill's evidence and of something Walter Tanner had said. Then he thought of Clive's divided loyalties and his obsession with time. He knew who had killed Dorothea Cassidy.

Now he was left with the problem of what to do with Emily Bowman. He could hardly ask her to promise, as Dorothea had done, not to kill herself. Emily Bowman seemed to guess what he was thinking.

"Don't worry, Inspector," she said. "The moment's past. I won't do anything melodramatic. At least not tonight."

He paused. The last thing he wanted was to offend her. "Does this treatment, which causes the discomfort, go on indefinitely?"

"No," she said. "Thank God. Only two more weeks."

"It might be better," he said, "to postpone a decision until then."

193

"So it might," she said, and smiled at him.

"Would you like company" he asked.

She smiled again. "Yes," she said. "Send Annie in to see me. She can make me some of her dreadful tea and talk about the men in her life."

Outside, it seemed hotter, more humid. When he swung open the double-glazed door from Armstrong House to the street, it was quite noisy, too. From across the river there was traditional fairground music and a siren which blew every time one of the rides reached a climax of speed. Occasionally a woman's scream tore through the background sound. By now the carnival parade would be over, the floats drawn up on the abbey meadow in a circle like a Wild West wagon train. The participants would be dispersing to the fair and the pubs. Soon the whole senseless performance would be over for another year.

Ramsay sat in the car and spoke urgently into the radio to Hunter. They would need a search warrant, he said. They might have some trouble with a conviction without Dorothea's diary and handbag, and he thought he knew where they might be found. Only then did he tell Hunter who they were looking for. He gave the sergeant no time for questions.

"Bring them both in," he said. "I have to speak to them both."

He left his car where it was, in Armstrong Street, close to Walter Tanner's front door. Perhaps I should speak to him, he thought. Check the details first. But he knew by now how desperate the murderer had become and that there was no time. It would be impossible to park in the centre of Otterbridge. This was as close as he could hope to get, so he walked down the quiet street toward the small gate which led to the park.

The policeman on duty there seemed surprised to see him, but recognised him and let him through without a word. There was no one else about. The respectable elderly residents had their curtains drawn against the noise and everyone else would be in town. The festival gave a legitimate excuse for them to drink too much, for rowdy exhibitionism. They would tell each other that it was tradition.

At almost the same time the night before, Dorothea Cassidy had been carried down this path and laid to rest on the flower bed. The park was as quiet now, at ten o'clock, with the pubs still open, as it would be in the early hours of the morning. There were lamps in the park, but they were a long distance apart and it was not, after all, so surprising that the revellers, on their way home in the dark, had failed to see a body at their feet.

The belief that Dorothea had been moved to the park in the early hours of the morning had been his first mistake. There had been many more. He had thought the murderer would be rational, clear-sighted, and realised now that each move had been a response to panic. He had to get to the town before the killer panicked again.

19

I_t had seemed to get dark suddenly. The sun disappeared and almost immediately afterwards the fairy lights along the river were switched on and the spotlights directed at the abbey and the town walls. The visitors who were climbing into coaches to take them home were enchanted. How pretty the town was! they said. What a delightful evening!

In contrast, with nightfall the fair became a more menacing and exciting place. Children were taken home, protesting and exhausted, carried on parents' shoulders, and the site was left to gangs of teenagers, to the older men who stood in the shadows and watched them jealously, and to the police with their photos and their questions. The rides seemed to become more noisy and frantic.

Joss Corkhill had spent all evening successfully avoiding the police. His friends on the fair had helped him, allowing him to crouch beneath the Hoop-la stall or in the canvas folds of the hot-dog tent. It had become a game—spotting the plainclothes detectives at a distance and making sure Joss was out of the way before they arrived at the ride where he was working. None of them had any time for the police. They had been harassed too often, blamed for crimes they had never committed. Now they felt the concentration of the police on the fairground was an injustice. Anyone in the town could have murdered that vicar's wife, they said. Why blame it on one of us? We didn't even know her, and old Joss wouldn't hurt a fly.

Joss had been drinking all evening and had reached the euphoric peak which was the highlight and purpose of all his drinking bouts. He did not always achieve the high, and he knew it would be quickly followed by depression, but while it lasted he was magnificently content. He wondered now how he had ever become entangled with Theresa Stringer and her bloody family. Why had he wanted her to travel with him so much anyway? He was better on his own. As he played his strange game of hide-and-seek all over the fairground, he felt the exhilaration of the chase. Nothing else had any importance at all.

He was back at work on the Noah's Ark when he saw the pretty woman who had been at the fair the night before with Dorothea Cassidy. He was standing on the ride with his back to the safety rail, keeping an eye on the crowd for the fuzz. Despite the alcohol, he balanced perfectly, even when the ride was at its fastest. He knew the two giggling girls sitting near to him were watching him, and he intended, as the ride slowed, to offer to help them off. Then he glimpsed the pale young woman, just for a moment, in the crowd. He was tempted to find one of the policeman, to point her out and say: "That's the one you want." But why should he? Let the police do their own dirty work.

Imogen Buchan did not know why Patrick had brought her to the fair. The noise and the crowd made her feel sick and faint. She had eaten very little all day. Patrick's phone call had summoned her to a pub in the town centre, close to the church, and she had thought they would talk, there would be explanations, and the tragedy of Dorothea's death would bring them close together again. There would be a return of the old intimacy. She would help him through his grief. Instead he

197

had dragged her from one packed pub to another, and when she tried to take his hand, to express some sympathy, he pushed her away. Then he had insisted that she go with him to the abbey field.

"I should go home," she had said. "They'll be wondering where I am. They'll be worried."

"Sod them!" he had said, and pulled her roughly by the arm, past the carnival floats over the dark and trampled grass to the fair. She had never liked the speed of the big rides. Even the galloping horses made her feel sick, she said, trying to make a joke of it, trying to lighten his mood. But he would not listen to her. He pulled her with him into the waltzers and sat with his arm around her, his fingernails dug into her shoulder, his head very close to hers. He seemed to take a delight in her terror, smiling when she screamed. Then he took her onto the Big Wheel. She gripped the safety rail and shut her eyes. The chair rose slowly as other riders got on beneath them. When they reached the highest point of the circle, he rocked the chairs violently, so she was certain he would tip them both out.

The centre of the town was so choked with traffic that Hilary Masters decided to park her car at the social services office. It would be easier to walk to her flat in a new block close to the river. The fresh air seemed to make Theresa more alert, but Hilary walked close beside her, protectively. It took longer than she had expected to reach the town centre; she had forgotten that the park had been closed to the public. When they got there, the carnival parade was already over and she was unreasonably upset that she could not show Theresa the decorated lorries.

"Never mind," she had said, as if speaking to a child. "There's always next year."

"I want to find Joss," Theresa said as they crossed the bridge. "I'm going to the fair to find Joss."

198

"I'm not sure that's a good idea," Hilary said dispassionately.

"I'm going to find Joss," Theresa repeated. "If you don't come with me, I'll go by myself."

So Hilary followed Theresa onto the field. She hadn't been to the fair since she was a child. It wasn't her scene. The place seemed fraught with danger and she looked, with her social worker's disapproval, at two kids who were clowning around at the top of the Big Wheel.

When it got dark, Edward Cassidy could stand waiting for his son no longer. He knew sleep would be impossible. He could not bear to shut the curtains because he wanted to catch the first glimpse of the headlights of Patrick's car, but the flashing lights of the fairground threw strange shapes on the walls and everywhere he thought he saw the shadow of Dorothea, laughing at him. He knew he was exhausted, but he knew, too, that he could not stay in the vicarage.

He left the light on in the hall and the door open and went outside. Even in the vicarage garden the noise overwhelmed him. The screech of machinery and of amplified pop music seemed unnaturally loud. He walked down the drive into the busy town centre and was swallowed up by the crowd. He saw everything in sharp outline, heard everything clearly—distinct phrases spoken by people he passed in the street, the strain of the Northumbrian pipes which came from an open pub window. He was watching and listening for Patrick, hoping to see the familiar lanky silhouette marching up the street in front of him, hoping to catch a few words spoken in a voice he recognised. He wanted to tell Patrick that they had both been fools.

In the small house in Armstrong Street Walter Tanner lay on his bed, wide-awake. The police had wanted him to move out for the night, had even suggested that they might put him up in a hotel if he had nowhere else to go, but with uncharacteristic spirit Walter had stood up to them. This was his

199

home, he said. Body or no body in the bath. Despite the horror of it all, he was happier here than anywhere else. He was too far from the fairground to be troubled by noise inside the house—he could hear the music but only faintly. Yet still he found it impossible to relax. Images whirled into his mind like the figures on a carousel. There was his mother, peevish and complaining, holding taut between her hands the wire she had used in the shop to cut the cheese; there was Dorothea, dressed as she had been on one of her visits to Walter in a white sleeveless sundress, held up only by thin straps at the shoulder; there was Clive Stringer, moronic and cunning, bent double with laughter. Walter got out of bed, walked to the window, and opened it, thinking some air might help him to sleep. As he pushed against the rusty catch there must have been a lull in the music, because when the window finally swung wide open, he quite clearly heard a woman scream, and then there was silence.

Ramsay walked quickly, but at the end of the bridge he stopped to call Hunter again to see if there was any news about the warrant.

"They've been seen!" Hunter said. He was very excited. "In the fair. But it's a madhouse in there and our blokes lost them in the crowd."

"That's all right," Ramsay said. "Pull all our people out and cover both ends of Front Street. They'll have to come that way and it'll be easier to get them on their way out."

"What do you want me to do?" Hunter asked. Ramsay knew he would like to be there for the arrest. He would hope for some dramatic chase so he could show off in front of the crowd.

"Supervise the search," Ramsay said. He sensed Hunter's disappointment but insisted. Hunter would be mercilessly thorough and he still thought they would need Dorothea's belongings to secure a conviction. "Get in touch if you find anything."

Suddenly he felt very tired. He longed for it all to be over. The whole town, it seemed, was a madhouse. Two women in fancy dress walked towards him in the middle of the road. Each had an arm around the other's shoulders, and they did a shuffling dance which ended when they collapsed into giggles. Somewhere, someone was singing "The Blaydon Races," tunelessly, very loud.

He walked on, ignoring his own advice, and pushing through the crowd onto the fairground. On the dodgems boys in black leather did battle in earnest silence, leaning forward over the driving wheels, bracing themselves for the shock of collision. The cars squealed as the boys braked and turned and blue sparks cracked at the end of the power lines. Some of the smaller stalls and the roundabouts for young children were being dismantled, but the crowd seemed reluctant to leave. Still people queued to ride the Pirate Ship, the waltzers, and the Big Wheel, and while they were prepared to pay, the fair stayed open. Ramsay stood by the Pirate Ship, scanning the faces, and watched as it began to swing, at first slowly like a large version of an old-fashioned swinging boat, then more deeply in sickening plunges until it made a complete revolution. He turned away, no longer interested, certain that there was no one on the ride he recognised.

Ramsay saw the two figures at the top of the Big Wheel from a distance, and he thought at first that they were children, messing about. He wondered angrily what sort of parents allowed their bairns to be out at a time like this, then thought that he had no right to judge. If he and Diana had produced children, they would probably have been uncontrollable. He walked on, moving backwards and forwards over the litter-strewn grass to cover as much ground as possible, vaguely aware that the Big Wheel was moving, but scanning the crowd at head height. He came back to the Big Wheel from a different angle just as it was stopping again.

The operator, a short, square man with huge hands was shouting.

"Last ride, please, ladies and gentlemen. Last ride."

And there was a jostle in the queue as they all pushed forward, anxious not to miss out. Very slowly the wheel moved round to allow people off two at a time and the new riders on.

Ramsay walked down the length of the queue, looking at the faces, then began to move away, thinking he would join his colleagues in Front Street. He had an irrational fear that without his supervision they would make a mess of the arrest.

When he heard the showman shout, "Take care, ladies and gentlemen. Don't push," he glanced back briefly. There was a skirmish at the front of the queue. Two teenage boys had been pushing for first place and the struggle had got out of hand. One of them had a cut lip. Their friends pulled them apart and Ramsay might have walked on when his attention was caught by the same two figures on the Big Wheel he had seen earlier, only as silhouettes. Now he could see them in detail and he recognised them immediately. They would be the last people to get off the ride and still their chair had not reached the peak of the circle. As he watched, it rocked violently and he knew that this was no children's game of dare.

He moved to see more clearly. Theresa Stringer had her hands around Hilary Masters's throat and was trying to force her backwards, out of the chair. Hilary's knees were caught under the safety rail but her back was arched beyond the back of the chair, and each time Theresa rocked, it seemed inevitable that the social worker would fall.

Nobody else had seen what was going on. The drama was taking place above their heads, beyond their line of vision. They were too eager not to miss the last chance for a ride to look about them. Ramsay shouted, but with the fairground noise, nobody heard. He rushed toward the operator, push-

202

ing his way through the crowd. They thought he was trying to jump the queue and stood together, shoulder to shoulder, menacing, and would not let him through. He waved and pointed and they thought he was drunk. In his panic he had lost all his authority.

The Big Wheel moved round again and Theresa and Hilary, still struggling, swung to the highest point of the circle.

Then, perhaps because someone in charge had decided that they could flout the byelaws no longer, that the evening would have to end soon, the music was switched off. In the silence that followed, Hilary's scream came as clear and sharp as a whistle, and everyone turned to watch, straining their necks in an effort to look up, as if this was some free entertainment to end the show. Ramsay thought it was like witnessing some dreadful pornography: the women locked in combat, their skirts pulled round their thighs, scratching and tearing at each other's hair and faces, and the crowd breathless, excited, aroused by the possibility of tragedy. For a moment the showman stood, entranced, as if he were waiting for Hilary to fall at last. Then Ramsay swore at him and he pulled a lever and the wheel moved jerkily round until the women had reached the ground.

"They must be pissed," someone in the crowd said. "Lasses shouldn't drink. They can't take it."

That seemed to relieve the tension and the people moved away, realising that there was no chance now for a last ride.

Hilary still sat in the chair, her head in her hands, crying. Theresa jumped out furiously. She was like a cat, spitting and clawing, and would have gone for the social worker again if the showman had not pulled her off. He stood, holding her from behind by the elbows, and she was so small and frail that she hardly reached the ground. Ramsay's radio buzzed and cracked and Hunter's triumphant voice cried out:

"We've found them. Just where you said they'd be. We've got her now."

Yes, Ramsay thought sadly. We've got her now.

He walked up to the two women. "Hilary Masters," he said, not looking at her. "I'm placing you under arrest. I must ask you to come with me to the police station."

He put his hand on her shoulder and felt the silk of her blouse and the bone underneath and thought he had been wanting to touch her all day.

20

He sat with her in the interview room. There was a woman constable sitting in a corner, her knees primly together, her hands on her lap, but they took no notice of her. They were like lovers in a crowded street, so caught up with each other that they can see no one else.

"She can't understand," Hilary said. "I only did it for her."

"Theresa?" he said. "You're talking about Theresa?"

She nodded. She wanted to explain.

"It didn't seem fair," she said, "to rake it up after all this time."

"To rake what up?" he asked, though he had guessed.

"The baby," she said. "Nicola."

"It wasn't a cot death?"

She shook her head. "Theresa smothered her," she said.

"Tell me what happened."

"The baby was in her cot. She was a difficult child and Theresa didn't have the patience to cope with her. She put a pillow over her head and smothered her. Then she phoned me. When I got there, she was sitting on the stairs, weeping. The baby wouldn't stop crying, she said. She had to make it stop crying."

205

Hilary spoke flatly, with the same detachment as she had in her office.

"You didn't tell the police?" he said.

She shook her head. "I was young," she said. "Not very experienced. I thought I'd get the blame. And I didn't want Theresa to go through all that, the court case, the publicity. Even if they didn't send her to prison, I didn't want her to have to go through all that. And it was my fault. I should have seen how desperate she was. She'd asked me to visit the day before and I'd been too busy to go. I felt responsible."

"So you covered it up?"

She shrugged. "I didn't mean to cover it up. I didn't want to be the one to give her away, but I thought there would be a postmortem. I thought they would discover then that it wasn't a natural death, but apparently it isn't that easy to detect."

"Weren't you worried that Theresa might turn on Beverley in the same way?"

"No!" she said sharply. It was as if he were questioning her professional judgement. "Really I wasn't. Theresa had matured a lot in that time. Clive was grown up and she could give all her attention to the baby. And I gave the case to Mike Peacock. He's young, but he's a very competent social worker. Then, as soon as there was a hint that the child was being abused, I took her into care."

So, Ramsay thought, that explained the speed with which the child was removed from the family. And the haste had made Dorothea suspicious and had led to her death.

"When did Dorothea find out about Nicola?" he asked.

"Yesterday afternoon," she said. "You knew she went back to the Stringers in the afternoon?"

"Yes," he said. "I think we have Dorothea's movements for the afternoon worked out quite precisely now, thank you."

206

It was as if she were still a colleague and they were working together to get at the truth.

"Theresa was upset," Hilary said. "She'd come to terms with the fact that if she wanted Beverley back, she'd have to give up any idea of going away with Joss Corkhill. That made her depressed. And then Dorothea was suspicious. 'I can't quite understand why Miss Masters is so keen to take Beverley away from you, Theresa. I think there must be something you haven't told me. How can I help you if you won't tell me the truth?' "

"So Theresa told her," Ramsay said.

"How could she help it? I've explained that she was already depressed, feeling sorry for herself. You don't know what Dorothea was like."

I think I do, Ramsay thought. I feel as if I've spent all day with her.

"How did you find out that Theresa had confessed to Dorothea?" he asked.

"Theresa phoned me from a call box on the Ridgeway. She was hysterical. At first I couldn't work out what had happened. It was like the time she phoned me after Nicola died."

"Did you look for Dorothea?"

"No," she said. "I waited for her to come to me. I knew she would be in touch." She looked at him. "I didn't have any plan," she said. "It wasn't in any way premeditated."

"How did Dorothea get in touch with you?"

"She turned up at my flat," Hilary said. "The waiting was awful. I had expected her earlier. She said there had been something urgent she'd had to attend to. Some family business."

She had been in the vicarage, Ramsay thought, with Patrick Cassidy, trying to persuade him, perhaps, that he did not love her after all, trying to fend off his teenage passion.

"What time did she come to the flat?"

"I'm not sure. At about seven."

"She had an appointment to speak to the Armstrong House Residents' Association at half-past. Didn't that bother her?"

"She tried to phone them to cancel it," Hilary said, "but she couldn't get through. She thought the phone was out of order." She paused. "I'd disconnected it. I had no plan to kill her then—it wasn't that I was covering my tracks—but I was afraid she might phone someone else, tell them about Nicola. I wasn't thinking very clearly."

"What did you do then?"

"I made her tea," she said. "We talked."

"About the baby?" he said.

She nodded. "She spoke as if we'd meant to kill Nicola," she said. "She went all religious on me. She even began to cry."

"Did you know," he said, "that she'd never been able to have children of her own?"

She shook her head. "No," she said. "I didn't realise. But I've never had the chance of children either. It didn't give her the right to preach." She paused. "I had the feeling that she wanted something from me," she said. "Some show of remorse. Repentance, I suppose she would have called it. I couldn't give it. I knew that in the same situation I would probably do exactly the same again."

"What did you do then?" he asked.

"She said she was hungry. She would take me out for a meal. Her treat. It seemed bizarre. We'd been arguing for more than an hour and she wanted to share a meal with me. I asked her about the appointment at Armstrong House, but she said it didn't matter. This was more important. We left her car outside my flat and walked through the fairground to that Italian place in Newgate Street."

"You were seen," he said, "in the fairground. Joss Cork-hill saw you. But when he described you, I thought he was talking about someone else. It never occurred to me that he wouldn't recognise you. Then I realised that senior social workers don't often work directly with clients. That's how I knew.''

There was silence. The policewoman moved slightly on her chair in the corner. She gave no indication that she was listening to the conversation and stared out at the shiny cream walls with blank boredom.

Then Hilary continued, although he had not asked a direct question.

''The restaurant was packed,'' she said, ''and very noisy. It took us ages to get served. Dorothea ordered spaghetti and ate it very neatly, twisting it between her fork and her spoon. She seemed ravenous. She insisted that I have a meal, too, though I wasn't hungry. I had expected another lecture, but still she didn't mention Nicola once. She talked, I remember, about friendship. When we left the place, it was almost ten.''

''Did you walk back through the fair?''

''No. We went the long way round, down the end of New-gate Street. When we got to the flat, I expected her to get into the car and drive away. It hadn't even crossed my mind then that I might kill her. She had been a social worker and I didn't think that she could really let loose all that publicity. She would know what would be likely to happen: the tabloid press, the MPs screaming for my blood, the witch-hunt that would affect everyone working for social services. I thought I could make her understand.

''Then at the car she began to start again. She made me get into the passenger seat. 'I can't let you go,' she said, 'until I've got some sort of commitment.' ''

''What did she want?'' he asked.

''My resignation,'' she said. ''I think, in the end, that's what she wanted.''

''Where did you kill her?'' he asked in the same tone of mild interest.

''In the car,'' she said. ''She was going on and on, not

shouting, you know. She never shouted. But somehow relentless. I wanted to stop her talking. I put my hands round her neck, just to show her how strongly I felt about it. As soon as she went quiet I stopped. But then I realised it was too late. She was dead. Theresa must have felt exactly the same when she killed the baby.''

''What did you do then?''

''I panicked,'' she said. ''I ran out into the street. I wanted to get right away from the body while I worked out what to do. If I'd run into a policeman, I'd have told him everything. But I ran into Clive Stringer. He'd been to the fair, spent all his money, and was hanging around on the corner of Newgate and Front Street, hoping, I think, for trouble.

''You got him to move the body for you?''

She nodded. ''I told him that Theresa had killed Dorothea, because she had wanted to stop her going away with Joss Corkhill.''

So he had been asked to choose, Ramsay thought, between Dorothea and his mother, and he had chosen, then at least, to protect Theresa.

''Was it hard to persuade him?'' he asked.

''Not very hard,'' she said. ''He was quite excited, you know, at the prospect of driving the car.''

''Did you tell him where to put the body?''

She shook her head.

''I told him to put it somewhere quiet, where it wouldn't be found until morning.''

''And presumably it was his idea to park the car in Walter Tanner's drive?''

She nodded. ''I didn't know anything about that until today. Apparently the old man didn't like him. It was Clive's way of paying him back.''

''Did you go with Clive to the park?''

''No,'' she said. ''I just wanted him to get rid of Dorothea. I suppose I wanted to pretend that I wasn't involved. I took

210

Dorothea's diary and handbag—I thought she might have made some record of her conversation with Theresa—then I left Clive to it. He must have driven to the little entrance of the park and carried her from there to the path by the river. He was quite remarkably strong. Then presumably he put the car on Tanner's drive.''

"He must have driven around a bit first," Ramsay said. "He didn't go down Armstrong Street until later."

"He was always into cars," she said. "It must have been a temptation to go joyriding."

"Why did you kill him?" Ramsay asked.

"He was nervous, stupid. I thought in the end he would tell someone. He was already feeling guilty. He loved Dorothea."

"You had a spare key to Tanner's house," Ramsay said, "because the home help service is organised from your office and Walter's mother had a home help. What happened to all the old keys? Were they labelled and left for collection?"

She nodded. "In the general office," she said. "It seemed too good an opportunity to miss. I thought if Clive were found in Tanner's house, you'd be bound to suspect the old man."

"How did you know Tanner wouldn't come in and surprise you?"

"I didn't," she said. "I took the risk. By then I was past caring. When I'd dropped you off at the police station, I drove toward Armstrong House. Clive had said he was on his way to work. I picked him up and offered him a lift."

"How did you get him into Tanner's house?"

"I told him to come with me," she said. "And he came. He was used to doing as he was told, and he was used to not understanding what was going on."

"Clive Stringer's death was premeditated," he said.

"Yes," she said. "I suppose it was."

There was a silence.

211

"You took off his watch when you cut his wrists," he said. "It was a mistake. You put it back in his room, didn't you, when you went to look after Theresa? I didn't remember until later that Clive never took off the watch because it was a present from Dorothea. It was obvious then that either you or Theresa had killed him—how else could the watch have been returned to his room? I didn't think it would be Theresa."

"She tried to kill me at the fair," Hilary said.

"Are you surprised?" he cried. "You killed her son."

For the first time the pretence that they were equals on some impersonal quest for facts was broken. She stared at him.

"I did it for her," she said. "I did it to protect her."

He wanted to contradict her, to tell her that she was deluding herself and that it had been her own reputation and safety she was concerned about, but he thought better of it. If she were to survive the court case and the prison sentence, she would need to believe that her motives, at least, were unselfish. He returned to the facts.

"When did Theresa realise?" he said.

"When we got to the fair. She'd been too drugged before then to think clearly. She wanted to look for Joss, but when we got there, she seemed distracted. There were two kids messing about on the Big Wheel. It must have given her the idea. She asked if we could have a ride. She seemed so keen that I agreed. Then she tried to push me out."

"We would have arrested you anyway," he said. "Even if she hadn't caused the scene."

"Yes," she said. "I see that now."

She seemed suddenly very tired. She lay her head on her arms like a child at its desk. He stood up quietly and walked out.

When Patrick Cassidy and Imogen returned to the vicarage, Edward was already there. They could see him in the bright, unflattering light of the study through the uncurtained window and hesitated on the gravel drive before going in to face him. For the first time it was cool and quiet. There was a breeze from the river. They had walked down the drive in silence, but now Patrick whispered: "I'm sorry about tonight. I don't know what came over me."

She did not know what to say. She was so tired, so lightheaded, that she felt nothing, not even relief that he seemed to be himself again. She took his hand and they went into the house. Edward must have heard the kitchen door being opened and he rushed to meet them.

"Patrick!" he said. "Thank God. Imogen, my dear child, you must phone your parents. They're worried sick. They've even been to the police. Sit down. You both look exhausted. Have you left the car in town? How sensible! We'll fetch it tomorrow. Let me make some tea."

He bustled about, his pleasure at seeing them shining through his grief. The phone rang.

"I expect that will be your parents to see if there's any news," he said. Then, as Imogen stood up to answer it: "No, no, you stay there. You look worn-out. You mustn't move. I'll tell them you can stay the night in the spare room and you can go home tomorrow."

He hurried from the room. The kettle began to hum. Imogen stood up, rinsed old tea bags from the pot, found new ones in a rusty tin caddy. After the evening of frantic activity, Patrick was drained, but calmer, almost relaxed.

"I'm sorry," he said again. "I was so angry. I needed to do something. I shouldn't have taken it out on you."

Before she could reply, Edward Cassidy came in. He was serious, rather dignified.

"That was Ramsay," he said. "The detective inspector. They've caught Dorothea's murderer. He wanted to tell me, he said, before I heard through the press. Apparently it was a social worker, some woman Dorothea had worked quite closely with. He didn't give me many details, but she's admitted everything. It's a relief, isn't it, it's over?''

Imogen looked at Patrick. He showed no reaction, seemed to feel no need for apology. You thought it might be me, she wanted to say. That's what all that was about tonight. You wanted to see if you could make me confess. But she said nothing. There had been enough drama for one day.

"I think I'll phone my parents," she said, "ask them to come and fetch me. I'd rather be at home."

"Can I see you tomorrow?" Patrick asked, but she did not answer. She needed time to think.

When Hunter and Ramsay left the police station, it was beginning to get light. They could see the silhouette of the abbey ruins against the grey sky. A lorry, towing a large caravan, rumbled out of the fairground, and many of the rides had already been demolished. They must have worked all night at it. The men did not speak. Ramsay had shown Hunter a copy of Hilary Masters's statement, but there was none of the jubilation that usually followed an arrest.

Poor bastard, Hunter thought. He really fancied her. He really fancied the Snow Queen.

In the car park they hesitated awkwardly, each standing by his car, unwilling to move away first.

"Look," Hunter said suddenly. "Why don't you come back with me? Have some breakfast. My mam's a great cook."

He did not for a moment think Ramsay would accept. They had nothing in common and had been rivals since Hunter had joined the team. Ramsay was too stuck-up, he thought. He was used to grander things. But the inspector smiled.

"Thank you," he said, knowing that Hunter had only

asked because he felt sorry for him, but grateful all the same. "If it wouldn't put your mother out too much, I'd like that."

He was not ready yet to face the empty cottage in Hepple-burn.

About the Author

The daughter of a village school teacher, Ann Cleeves lives in Nathumberland, England, where she spends her time with her two small children and writing.

A Day in the Death of Dorothea Cassidy is her seventh novel. She is also the author of *A Bird in the Hand*, *Come Death and High Water*, *Murder in Paradise*, *A Prey to Murder*, *A Lesson in Dying*, and *Murder in My Backyard*.

ANN CLEEVES
writes mysteries
like you've
never read before!